Jo Macauley

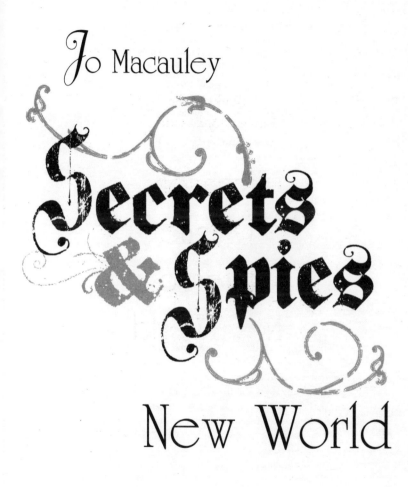

Secrets
&
Spies

New World

With special thanks to Adrian Bott

First published in 2013 by Curious Fox,
an imprint of Capstone Global Library Limited,
7 Pilgrim Street, London, EC4V 6LB
Registered company number: 6695582

www.curious-fox.com

Text © Hothouse Fiction Ltd 2013

Series created by Hothouse Fiction
www.hothousefiction.com

The author's moral rights are hereby asserted.

Cover design by samcombes.co.uk

ISBN 978 1 78202 043 1

1 3 5 7 9 10 8 6 4 2

A CIP catalogue for this book is available from the British Library.

Typeset in Adobe Garamond Pro by Hothouse Fiction Ltd

Printed and bound by CPI Group (UK) Ltd, Croydon, CRO 4YY

For Beatrice

# Prologue

## London, October 1666

The ship's name was *Dreadnought*, but that name no longer suited her. To look at the state she was in as she lay moored in Portsmouth harbour, you would think the tattered hulk would have a good deal to dread. The ship's carpenter had done the best he could to patch her up, but his repairs looked like make-up on a week-old corpse. If the wind blew too sudden and strong, the mainmast would topple like a rotten old oak. The boards were split below the waterline, and tarred rags could only keep the sea out for so long.

Her captain, Hugh Tucker, didn't look too healthy

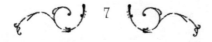

himself. In a dockside inn not far from where his ship was berthed, he sat across the table from a fat man in a wig. Candlelight lit Tucker's face from below, turning it into a gaunt, bearded skull.

"I don't like this job, and I don't like you," Tucker said. He was on his third cup of wine, and it had freed his tongue from politeness.

"You aren't being paid to like either," the fat man said. "My employer is paying you to take his ship where he wants it to go, carrying the cargo he chooses to export."

"Cargo!" Tucker shook his head in disgust.

The fat man shrugged. "A commodity like any other."

"You call a hold full of prisoners a commodity?"

"Don't tell me you've developed a conscience." Lucius Bebbington, the fat man, sounded bitter and bored. He took a large fingerful of snuff. "It doesn't suit you, Captain Tucker. Not with your reputation."

"It's not that!" Tucker grimaced. "And it's not the money, either. The money's good enough. But your employer wants me to pack 'em in like so much stovewood!"

"The *Dreadnought* is a large ship," Bebbington pointed out.

8

"But three hundred? It'd be like piloting Newgate Prison across the blasted Atlantic."

"The more prisoners we can ship to America, the more the government will pay. It's sound economic sense."

"And if we never reach America?" Tucker said, glowering over the candle. "What then? Look, you've seen the state of the *Dreadnought*. That storm off Penzance practically crippled her."

"She's seaworthy enough."

"If your mysterious employer would just fork out for repairs…"

"Oh, let's not open *that* casket of worms again." Bebbington rolled his eyes. "If you'd kept to the agreed course, you'd never have run into that storm in the first place."

"I told you, the Dutch would have been on us if I hadn't!"

"My dear captain, calm down. Do you want everyone to know our business?"

Tucker filled a pipe with shaking hands. Bebbington watched impassively while he lit it.

"It ain't like we'd be transporting cattle nor coal," Tucker protested. "These are criminals. They outnumber the crew! What if there's an escape, a mutiny?"

"It's your job to make sure there isn't one."

"And you're overloading a damaged ship! The weight of that many people … If we run into another storm…"

Bebbington leaned over the table. "Don't quote me, but I'm sure my employer won't mind if you throw one or two overboard," he whispered. "Lightens the load *and* serves as a warning to the others. Two birds with one stone, eh?"

Captain Tucker looked sick.

Bebbington stood up abruptly. "You have your orders," he said. "The *Dreadnought* will sail on the fourteenth, as agreed. Oh, cheer up, damn you! This time next year, you will be a rich man."

Tucker swept his hat onto his head. "Your obedient servant, *sir*," he said. He stumbled out of the inn without a backward glance.

The night was cold and a sea mist had drifted in. It quickly leeched away what little warmth the wine he'd drunk had provided. Tucker pulled his coat around him and cursed the weather, the sea, that fat pig Bebbington, and his blasted employer most of all.

Up ahead, the looming shape of the *Dreadnought* made Tucker shiver even more. He thought of three hundred convicts crammed into that fragile wooden

hull. Desperate sorts, all of them. Thieves. Beggars. Scum with nothing to lose.

Suddenly he was very afraid.

"Damned souls," he whispered hoarsely to himself. "And me the captain of the ship chartered to take them down to Hell…"

Meanwhile, back at the inn, Bebbington was welcoming a colleague to his table.

"You talked him round, then?" the man asked. "I thought he was going to swing at you for a moment."

"Men of the sea are like dogs," Bebbington said with a tight smile. "They're not happy unless you keep them in their place. Whip 'em once in a while. Show 'em who's boss."

"He'll sail?"

"He must. And he knows it."

"Then here's to prosperity," the man said, raising his glass. "Gold uncounted. Riches galore."

"A fair wind, a calm sea, and hundreds of golden guineas in the bank," Bebbington agreed.

They clinked glasses and drank.

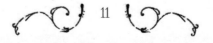

Bebbington smacked his lips. "I can't wait to tell Mister Vale the good news. He'll be so pleased with the two of us!"

# Chapter One

## Voice from the Shadows

At the Theatre Royal, Drury Lane, the actors of the King's Company were in the front row of seats, looking up at an empty stage.

Beth Johnson could hardly sit still for excitement. Her green eyes sparkled with anticipation and she played with her long braid of chestnut-brown hair impatiently. Soon William Huntingdon, the company's manager, would appear and deliver the news that everyone was waiting to hear. Only her arch-rival, Benjamin Lovett, was refusing to get into the spirit of things.

"Get *on* with it," he groaned, rolling his eyes.

"The sooner it's announced, the sooner we can get on to the important business!"

"The casting?" Beth said.

"Naturally, the casting," Lovett sniffed. "I wouldn't get too giddy about it if I were you, though. There aren't many women's parts in … well, let's just say I've heard it may be a famous Roman play."

"It's *Julius Caesar*, then, is it?" piped up one of the younger actors.

"I'm not at liberty to say," Lovett said, idly examining his nails. "But this theatre will certainly benefit from a touch more serious drama and a little less buffoonery!"

Beth decided to ignore Lovett's predictions. He always acted as if he was privy to everything that went on in Huntingdon's office, but the truth of it was he didn't have any more of a clue than anyone else in the company.

Also, he was bitterly jealous of Beth.

She'd given him good reason to be jealous, these last few months. She had quite simply acted him off the stage in every single production. She had dazzled as Viola in *Twelfth Night*, brought the audience to tears as Helen of Troy, and made the rafters shake with laughter as the impish Queen Mab. It was Beth who the audience

 14

came to see and Lovett knew it. Granted, the audiences had been a little thin of late, but Beth knew she wasn't the cause. Buffoonery, indeed! Lovett could go hang, the pompous old ham. The theatre was meant to be fun, and after the horrors of the Plague and the Great Fire, these people needed more fun in their lives!

Whatever this new production might be, Beth knew she had a strong chance of landing the lead part – assuming it wasn't a male-dominated play like *Julius Caesar*. The best she could hope for from that one was Caesar's wife Calpurnia or Brutus's wife Portia. She wrinkled her nose at the thought. Huntingdon adored Shakespeare, true, and the audiences always lapped it up. But *that* play? A drama about a political murder, in the King's own playhouse? Lovett had to be bluffing, surely.

"Good afternoon, everyone!" Huntingdon said, striding onto the stage. Behind him came a stubbly-chinned man in a rather grubby shirt, holding a violin. A few gasps of surprise went up from the players.

"This is Mister Meecher," Huntingdon explained. The violinist nodded and gave a gap-toothed grin. "He will be assisting me today."

The players looked at one another, unable to work out what was going on. All Beth could think was:

*This doesn't look like Caesar to me.*

"You will all be aware," Huntingdon continued, "that our audiences have been smaller and smaller of late – no, no, let's not deny it, we all know it to be true – while the Duke's Theatre, our main competitors, are getting more bottoms on seats with every passing week!"

So *that* was where the vanishing audiences were going, Beth thought darkly.

"They are stealing from us," Huntingdon said frankly. "Not by pinching our scripts, though we know they've stooped to that level before. No – they're simply playing the game better. They're offering something the public want, something we aren't giving them. Well, I've had enough. And it's time we fought back!" His angry voice resounded from the back of the theatre. "Shakespeare!" he bellowed.

Beth groaned inwardly and her heart sank. So it was going to be *Julius Caesar*, after all. She glanced over and saw Lovett grinning smugly in her direction.

"The Duke's men outdid us with a Shakespeare production!" Huntingdon shouted, striding up and down the stage like a sergeant major. "I won't have it! Nobody puts on better Shakespeare plays than us, and yet their production of *The Tempest* is the talk of London."

He turned imploringly to his troupe. "And what, do you suppose, was the secret of their success?"

Nobody dared to answer.

"Music and songs!" he cried. "They made a big production out of every song in the play! Instead of the same old tunes from a hundred years ago, they used fresh music – *popular* music. I've come to a realization. Acting's not enough. People want singing too, and lots of it. We must rise to the challenge."

A new feeling of dread came over Beth at this. She'd rather have played a Roman matron than have to try for a singing part…

"Our next production," Huntingdon announced, "will be a new musical by Mister Thornwick, entitled *Robin of the Greenwood*. All the main parts are singing parts." Huntingdon grinned. "If you wish to be considered for a main part, then you'll need to sing! Auditions in five minutes, everyone."

Beth bit her lip. It wasn't that she didn't *like* singing. If she was on her own, she loved to sing. It was just that … well … nobody else liked to be around her while she did.

Everyone else was getting up and heading to the wings, waiting to be called on stage, while Huntingdon

made notes of their names. Beth sat where she was, her stomach churning. Maybe she should just let this one go, she thought. Would it really matter all that much if she didn't get a lead part, or even a large part? But she couldn't just back out. She had to try, even if the result was embarrassing. She took a deep breath and went to join the others.

*Usually*, auditions were exciting. Beth *usually* couldn't wait for her name to come up. This time, she lurked in the shadows in the wings, dreading the sound of her name on Huntingdon's lips. One by one he called the cast forward, letting them choose the song they wanted to perform. Mr Meecher, who seemed to know every song ever written, accompanied them on his violin to help them keep in tune.

When it was Lovett's turn, Beth shrank into herself even more. He had a fine tenor voice, she had to admit. One more thing for him to lord it over her about. He was always acting superior: around her, around the other actors and especially around poor young Maisie, the theatre's orange-seller and Beth's close friend and confidante…

Beth suddenly sat bolt upright in her chair. *Maisie!* She could sing; she could sing beautifully, in fact.

18

Often, when she was doing some little job or other in their lodgings she'd sing to herself, and Beth had always admired her friend's voice. The moment Lovett had finished, Beth ran onto the stage.

"Mister Huntingdon, can I ask a favour?"

Lovett looked at her sceptically. "Let me guess. She wants to jump the queue and go on next."

*You couldn't be more wrong*, Beth thought, but she ignored him. "It's about Maisie," she said to Huntingdon. "I know she's not really been on stage much, but she *is* part of the company, and she sings awfully well, so I thought maybe we could, well … let her audition?"

"An orange girl?" Lovett exploded before Huntingdon could speak. "You can't possibly be serious."

"If you don't recall, I started off as an orange girl at the theatre myself! Just give her a chance!" Beth said, irritated at his constant interjections. "She works hard. She deserves it!"

Huntingdon frowned. "I don't know, Beth. Maisie's got a good heart, true, but the stage isn't for everyone. We can't just throw it open to all-comers."

Beth thought quickly. "If we're going to beat the Duke's, we need the best singers we can get, don't we?"

"The best singers in the company, yes, but—"

"So how will you know how good she is unless you let her audition?" Beth gave Huntingdon her practised wide-eyed, pleading gaze. "What have you got to lose?"

Huntingdon thought about it, then shrugged. "I don't suppose it does any harm. Very well. I'll add her to the list."

Lovett sputtered like an old leaky kettle coming to the boil. "This theatre is going to the dogs!" he hissed. "No wonder we're losing audiences. We used to have standards, you know!" With that, he stormed off backstage.

Beth savoured her little moment of triumph over him. Her powers of persuasion were still as strong as ever. Just as well, considering her other secret line of work – the one nobody at the theatre even suspected. As a spy, she had to be able to talk people round. Working for the Crown under the guidance of spymaster Sir Alan Strange, she'd often needed to fall back on her acting talents to get out of tight scrapes or gather information. The skill had saved the King's life more than once – not to mention her own…

\* \* \*

Not long after, Maisie stood on the stage, wringing her hands nervously, her dark curls tumbling around her face. The rest of the cast looked on, willing to give her a chance. Most of them, anyway. Maisie glanced at Beth for reassurance. Beth smiled back, hoping against hope that she hadn't made a horrible mistake. If this ended with Maisie in tears, or if Lovett said anything cruel, she'd never forgive herself.

"What would you like to sing?" Huntingdon asked.

Maisie mumbled something. Beth's heart sank.

"Louder, please!"

"'The Girl I Left Behind'," Maisie said.

Meecher nodded and set his bow to the strings. Lovett sneered and Beth heard him mutter, "Irish tinker songs. Now I've heard it all."

But as Maisie began to sing, his mouth slowly fell open. It was the voice of an angel. The cast stopped talking and listened. Beth's smile grew broader. It was only a folk song, true enough, but Maisie made the homely melody into something beautiful. Her voice rang out pure and clear, growing in confidence as she sang. Huntingdon was nodding now, writing something on his paper and beginning to smile too. Maisie drew out the last, long shivery note, then stood blinking and

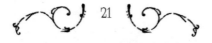

looking around her like a sleepwalker who had woken up. Immediately the whole cast broke out in applause. Some even shouted "Bravo!"

"Thank you, Maisie," Huntingdon said. "Thank you very much indeed."

Maisie ran straight to Beth in the wings, her blue eyes shining. "Did I do all right?"

"Oh, Maisie, you did fabulously!" Beth laughed, hugging her. She caught Lovett's eye and held his gaze, daring him to say something nasty. But to her surprise, he seemed to be regarding Maisie with something like awe, as if he'd had a vision.

"She's a pure soprano," he breathed. "I've never heard the like, not even in Venice. I ... I don't ... excuse me." He turned away and pulled a big white kerchief out of his sleeve. Beth couldn't believe it. Maisie's singing had brought Lovett to tears!

"Beth?" called Huntingdon. "Your turn."

Reality came crashing back upon her. Beth slowly walked onto the stage, feeling like she was heading to her execution. The happy faces and expectant smiles from the other players just made it worse.

"Um ... I'll do 'Greensleeves'," she mumbled.

The next five minutes were purgatory. She sang as low

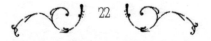

and quiet as she could, but her voice wouldn't do what it was supposed to. She did her best to hit the notes, but she just kept sliding off them. She tried to smile, since she'd been told that it helped the tune, but if anything it made her voice even more shrieking and off-key than before. Halfway through she saw the look on Huntingdon's face – the expression of a man who has been served a disgusting meal but is trying to keep a polite face. She tried to draw out the last note as Maisie had done, but the sound was like an outhouse door creaking shut.

Total silence followed.

The cast looked at one another. Beth's cheeks were on fire.

"Uh, thank you," Huntingdon finally managed to say. "I think that will be all."

Beth scuttled off into the wings, not daring to look back, and settled in the furthest, most shadowy corner she could find…

Blessedly the auditions were soon over, and Maisie and Beth sat together in the retiring room. Maisie was so excited at the prospect of being a part of the production

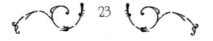

that Beth found she couldn't dwell too long on her own atrocious performance. Her friend's good mood was infectious.

"However did you learn to sing like that?" Beth asked her. "Even Lovett was impressed. That *never* happens."

"I've been singing as long as I can remember," Maisie smiled. "Since I was little, I mean. It started with the toil songs."

"Because your mother was a transportee?" Beth knew that Maisie had come over on the ships from America after her mother died. Ever since she'd arrived, she'd been keen to locate her father, whom she believed was somewhere in London.

Maisie nodded. "They made us work hard, all the girls and women," she said, without bitterness. "Every day, they drove us out onto the farms to harvest the tobaccy. It's hot work, Mistress Beth, and deathly dull too. The singing helped, made the day go by a little sweeter."

"But how old were you, when they started you to work?"

Maisie shrugged. "Soon as you were old enough to walk, you were old enough to lift a bundle. They sent us into the fields beside our mothers."

Beth gave Maisie's shoulders a spontaneous squeeze,

shocked. "That must have been very tough."

"I suppose," Maisie said. "But I got to see America. I wouldn't have missed that for anything!" She sighed. "You'd love it, Miss Beth. It's such a beautiful country, so open and green and free. Here in London there are so many people and everything costs so much and it always smells so bad … I sometimes lie awake at night and I think of America. One day I'll go back. I know I will."

Beth looked at her friend and smiled. She knew Maisie had come to London hoping that this was where her long-lost father was, but the love in her eyes for America made Beth hope Maisie got to go back there one day too…

# Chapter Two
**Burned**

The best thing to do about her disastrous singing audition, Beth decided, was to laugh it off. That way, perhaps she wouldn't cringe every time she thought about it. But it was much easier to laugh about things when you were telling the story to someone else, and with an unexpected wrench, Beth realized how much she'd missed her handsome friend and fellow spy, John Turner. They hadn't met in ages and she missed his smile, she thought with a blush. Since the two of them, along with former street urchin-turned-agent Ralph Chandler, had foiled the last plot on the King's life, the messages

from their spymaster Strange had fallen silent. At times like this their secret spying life seemed almost unreal, submerged under the day-to-day.

She wondered if she should set up a meeting herself. Beth knew she wasn't technically *supposed* to meet up with John unless they were working together, but surely she ought to, if only to check if he'd heard anything from Strange? It was good spycraft, she told herself, to make sure your fellow operatives were alive and well.

Yes. Smiling again now, she threw her cape over her shoulders. "Where are you off to, then?" Maisie called to her.

"Oh, just visiting a friend," Beth said airily.

Maisie raised an eyebrow. "Ask no questions, tell no lies!" She tapped her nose, winked and went back inside.

"Indeed," Beth murmured to herself as she set off.

Beth frowned as she approached the cobbled path near John's house. Something was out of place – what was it? She stood still for a moment, listening, observing. Then it struck her. The silence. John had a large family, she knew that. But no children were playing in the street,

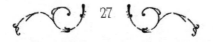

and no voices were whooping or arguing from inside. She rapped on the door with one of the coded knocks Strange's spies used. Three knocks, pause, then another.

John answered, and he looked surprised for a moment to see her, but the deathly look on his face made her own smile vanish.

"B— I mean, can I help you, miss?" he said, recovering his protocol.

Beth slipped effortlessly into character. "I'm so sorry to trouble you. My coach has lost a wheel out in the street and I need some strong arms to help lift the new one on. I don't suppose I could ask for your help? I'll pay, of course…"

John glanced back into the house and Beth could see from the doorway that much of his family was gathered in the kitchen: his mother and most of his brothers and sisters, including Polly, who needed crutches to walk. All of them looked grave. In the big chair in the corner of the room sat a man who must be John's father, Arthur, holding his right hand in a pottery bowl. As he lifted it out for a moment, Beth felt a shock as she saw it was bright red and inflamed.

"I'm just going to help this lady change a cartwheel," he called, and then quickly hurried out of the house.

"John, was that your father?" she said when they were around the corner.

John nodded, his face still pale and drawn. "He scalded himself at the ironworks and he's not able to work. It was an accident," he told her, quickly adding, "but it wasn't his fault. It could have happened to anyone."

They came to a halt and John sat heavily down on a nearby bench. Beth sat down beside him as he let out a huge sigh.

"It's bad, Beth."

She rested a hand on his arm. "My goodness, it sounds it…"

"There's no money," John continued. "I'm bringing home enough to pay the rent, but only just. My father's trying to put a brave face on it for Mother's sake and the children's, but he's eaten up with worry."

"He's healing, though, isn't he? Surely he'll be able to go back to work once he's better."

"We're treating it as best we can," John said. "Mother's been grinding up herbs in a pestle and making dressings. We all wanted to get him a proper doctor, but Father's boss wouldn't pay for one and we can't really afford one on our own…"

Beth knew what John meant. Doctors were expensive

and John's family was poor – and by the sounds of it much poorer now that their main breadwinner couldn't work.

"Talk to Ralph!" she said. "His landlord's an apothecary. Surely he can help?"

"I already did. It was Mister Culpeper who sold us the herbs, and at a generous discount too. Bear's breeches and coltsfoot. He says there's nothing better for a bad burn. Ivy leaves in wine would help keep it clean, but we don't have any wine in the house just now."

Beth wondered if John's house had *ever* had any wine in it.

"He's in a lot more pain than he lets on." John shook his head wearily. "The burn's deep. It's gone septic. The herbs are helping, I think, but it's so hard to tell. He won't admit how badly it hurts him, because he doesn't want us to worry."

"He's a good man," was all Beth could think of to say. *Just like his son.*

"Well, I'm not going to let him down," John said. "I've put in for extra hours at the Navy Board. It won't bring in much, but every penny matters. And I'm going to ask Strange for as much spywork as he can give me. I'll take anything…" He looked hopeful suddenly, remembering

Beth's visit was unexpected. "That's not why you're here, is it? You haven't heard from him?"

"No, no, I'm afraid not. I'd just come by to check in with you – and I'm glad I did." Beth's stomach lurched to hear him say he was hoping to make more money from spy work. They both knew that the more dangerous a mission was, the more Strange would pay. A sense of duty was all well and good, but the promise of hard cash made men brave too. And if a spy didn't survive, Strange would still make sure some money was passed to his family. He was very discreet about such things – there were families who still had no idea their loved ones had been working for him. So far as they knew, some mysterious nameless benefactor had helped them just when they most needed it.

"I'm glad too," John had been saying with a smile. He placed his hand on top of hers for a moment.

"Just be careful if you do speak to Strange for a new assignment," she warned. "It'd break your mother's heart if you were hurt too. Or worse…"

"You know what the Good Book says, Beth. '"He who does no work, neither shall he eat.'" He lowered his voice. "And my family really do need food. They won't go hungry. I won't let them."

 31

"I'll help any way I can," Beth promised. "Especially when it comes to spy work!"

John flashed her a grin. "Going to keep an eye on me, are you?"

*Finally, a glimpse of the old John*, she thought, returning his smile.

"Somebody has to," she quipped. "Can't have you getting into danger without me to back you up."

"To be honest, I'm not sure there *is* all that much danger right now. Strange hasn't told us anything new about Vale for ages. Do you suppose he's keeping us in the dark, or has that fiend finally given up in his attempts on the King?"

"It wouldn't be like Strange to lie to us. I think Vale really has just gone quiet."

The more Beth thought it over, the more certain she became. Like a hunted fox, Vale had gone to ground. Perhaps their efforts against the anti-royal conspirator and his men had finally paid off, and he was gone for good?

But as it happened, she couldn't have been more wrong.

# Chapter Three
## Old Acquaintance

The last person Beth expected to see waiting for her at the theatre was Sir Alan Strange. She had to do a double take. At first she thought she must have been mistaken. The Strange she knew was a craggy, ominous man who lurked in shadows, shrouded in a cape. This man was smartly dressed, with a pleated ruff and a luxurious wig. He was carrying a bunch of flowers.

"Ah, Miss Johnson," he said pleasantly. "I hope you don't mind. I'm an admirer. I bought these for you."

"How ... lovely," Beth said, accepting them while eyeing him closely. Her mind was racing. Strange must

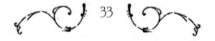

be here to tell her something, perhaps to warn her? She tried to look around without making it too obvious. This scene they were playing out had to look natural, in case anyone was watching.

"If it's not an intrusion, I'd love to talk to you about your acting. Might I presume to offer you a glass of sherry at my club?"

Beth swallowed. "That would be delightful."

Strange signalled to someone out of sight. Moments later a carriage came clattering to a halt beside them, as if he had conjured it from thin air. Strange opened the door and Beth ascended the step into the carriage's dark interior. He followed, and the driver set off without asking for directions. He already knew where he was going.

Strange's face changed the instant the door was closed. The simpering gentleman was gone and the gleaming-eyed hunter was back. "Not my preferred means of contacting you, but unfortunately there wasn't time to let you know I was coming."

"I understand," Beth said. "Did I—?"

"You performed passably well," Strange interrupted. "You didn't bluster, and you picked things up quickly."

"Thank you, sir."

"But next time a gentleman you don't know invites you into his carriage, try to protest a little more before agreeing. You have your reputation to think of…"

Beth's cheeks burned. She suddenly missed the days when Strange would summon his spies to St Paul's using the bells. Of course, those days were gone now. The Great Fire of London had gutted the cathedral, bell tower and all.

"I've an important assignment for you," Strange said. "We've had word. For some time now I've suspected Henry Vale was running a nest of agents right here in London. It looks like I was right."

"How certain are you?"

"Not certain enough, and that's why I need you. We *may* have tracked down Vale's base of operations here. Several of his known agents have been spotted going in and out of a particular building on the bank of the Thames. It's a tower, part of what's left of Richmond Palace."

Beth could hardly believe her ears. "Richmond Palace? Where the royal family used to live?"

"That was a long time ago, Beth. After the war, when the King had been murdered and Cromwell was in charge, the Parliamentarians had most of

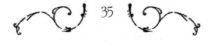

Richmond Palace torn down."

"Why?"

"Partly out of hatred of the monarchy and everything it stood for. But they had another, more important motive: greed. They sold the very stones Richmond Palace was built from."

Beth began to understand. It would suit Vale to live in the ruins of a royal palace, especially if his own side had had it destroyed. It would be like a constant reminder of his victory.

"Hardly anything of the old palace is left now," Strange continued. "The few remaining buildings were sold to private owners."

"One of whom could be Henry Vale using a false name."

Strange nodded. "Precisely. And for all we know, he may even be there in person."

Beth hardly dared to hope it might be true. The King-killer, holed up on their very doorstep, and they might even have one up on him. "So, do we break into that tower?"

"No." Strange's eyes flashed dangerously, then he closed them and became calm again. "Not yet. If we move too quickly we could scare him off and lose our

one chance to capture him. I want you to take part in an intensive surveillance operation."

As the carriage lurched through the London streets, bound for Heaven only knew what eventual destination, Beth listened while Strange explained the plan. She and some other agents would need to move into a safe house near the former palace and keep watch on the tower continually.

"And by that," Strange said, "I mean twenty-four hours a day, seven days a week. One of you must keep his or her eyes on that tower's front door at all times. If you need to eat, you wait for your break. If nature calls, you call on another agent to watch for you. No excuses. Do I make myself clear?"

*Unpleasantly so*, Beth thought. But then, that was Strange's way.

"Naturally, since this is a demanding mission, the rewards will be higher. You'll receive half again of your usual rate. Of course, if you can't leave the theatre for a week or so, I'm wasting my breath," Strange said. "Is it feasible you could make some excuse to be away?"

Beth's first thought was: *What about the new production? I'd never be able to take part.* Then it hit her. Missing this production, where all the main parts were singing parts,

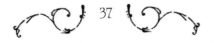

could be a blessing in disguise. Ever since her disastrous audition she'd been dreading Huntingdon's casting decision, knowing she would be relegated to some minor part. But if she told him she wasn't available, then neither of them needed to go through with it. It was a perfect way to save face. All she had to do was announce she was taking a holiday. Nobody could deny she'd worked herself to the bone over the last few weeks, could they? She was entitled to a break.

"Yes, it shouldn't be a problem," she said firmly.

"Excellent," Strange said. He passed her a slip of paper. "Details are here. The first shift should begin at sunset tonight. I'll assign you some other agents to work with."

"You'll ask John Turner, won't you?" Beth said.

Strange frowned. "Are you telling me how to do my job, Miss Johnson?"

"Ask him," Beth repeated firmly. For once, she didn't care how hard Strange glared at her. "He needs the money. If he's not in, then neither am I…"

\* \* \*

"Playing house!" Ralph Chandler muttered. "That's all we're doing here. Playing bloomin' house."

"You're only saying that because I'm beating you," Beth said with a grin at her fellow spy. She passed Ralph the dice. "Your turn."

"I'm sick of backgammon." Ralph stood up and stretched. "How long has it been now?"

"About fifteen minutes since the last time you asked," John said from the window. "Check the clock if you want to know the time."

He was sitting on a stool at the room's only window, watching the tower door through a strange tubular device with glass lenses in it. Strange had told them it had once belonged to Doctor Dee, the master spy and astrologer who had served Queen Elizabeth I. It was called a telescope. A large clock loomed over the room from the far wall, marking the hours of their shifts with its chimes, governing them like some stiff and humourless wooden avatar of Strange. Still, Beth couldn't help feeling quietly content to be back again with her colleagues – and good friends – on an assignment.

"Game of cards?" she suggested.

Ralph shook his head and went to join John at the window. "Look at that river. Teeming with fish, it is. I could pop down, catch us a nice fresh supper and be back before anyone knew."

"If you can't stand the waiting about," John snapped, "why'd you sign up for this?"

"Believe it or not, I'd missed your pretty faces," Ralph said with an arched eyebrow. "Even if you do keep thrashing me at cards. Oh, go on then, Beth. Let's have another round of cribbage."

*If it weren't for the tedium and for being stuck inside*, Beth thought, *this would be a nice relaxing holiday break.* She shuffled the deck of cards with practised skill, ready for another victory.

Their temporary base was "Merrybank", a boatman's cottage just downriver from Richmond Palace. The upper floor was a cramped attic room with sloping walls and a single window, and the three of them had made a nest of it. Cushions, books and the remains of meals lay around the floor. Strange had forbidden them to make any light in case it alerted the quarry, so their sole entertainments – card games and reading – had to stop at dusk when they ran out of light to see by. It made for long, boring nights.

From the window, they could clearly see the lonely tower that was under suspicion out among the ruins. One at a time, they had taken turns to watch the door, but so far nothing had stirred. Still, John had a pencil

and paper poised to note down anything they saw.

The first time Beth had seen the view from the upper window, the scale of the devastation had taken her breath away. She had dim memories of seeing Richmond Palace from the river as a child. It had been a place of high towers and turrets, a fairy-tale edifice looking out over the peaceful river to one side and the green hunting grounds of Richmond Park to the other. Like many little girls, Beth had dreamed of living there, like a princess. Now, in the advancing twilight, it looked like nothing could live there but ghosts. The high walls had completely gone, along with almost all of the towers and most of the chapel. The gatehouse was still intact, but without the palace to protect, it was a gate to nowhere. The few structures that remained jutted up from the ground like odd teeth.

Yes, Vale could easily live in a dismal place like this. But that didn't mean he *was* there. Time and again, Strange had taught her that only the facts mattered. They were here to find out those facts, not spin tales of skulduggery…

The grandfather clock solemnly tolled six, and they all looked up.

"That's your cue," Beth told Ralph. "Cards will

have to wait."

Ralph went to take John's place at the window. For all his complaining, he watched with the patience of a hunter when it was his turn. John came over and collapsed in a heap opposite Beth. He began to munch an apple. "I'm not sure I can take much more of this excitement," he said sarcastically. "My nerves are in tatters."

"How's your dad?" Beth asked. She hadn't wanted to say anything in front of Ralph, but she couldn't wait any longer. John glanced wearily up, and Beth wondered when he'd last had the chance to rest.

"He's no better. And that sack of guts," he checked himself, "his *boss*, Gaviston, has told him he hasn't a job to go back to even if he does heal up."

Beth stared, aghast. "He can't do that!"

"Of course he can. He has orders coming in, he says, and if they're not completed he'll lose trade, which he can't afford to do. So he's had to give my dad's job to someone else."

"That's horrible! Oh, John, I'm so sorry."

"'The ironworks isn't a charity', he says," John spat. "Anyway, there's no use in resenting it. I'm the man of the house now. Until the young 'uns are old enough to work, it's down to me to provide for my family."

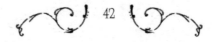

Beth's heart sank for him. It wasn't fair for so much responsibility to be dumped on her friend's shoulders. She could tell he was being brave, but the hope had gone out of his eyes. He was desperate now.

She reached out to him. "John, I—"

"Psst!" Ralph said. "Get over here, *now*!"

Quickly they scrambled to join him at the window. Even without Strange's telescope, Beth and John could clearly see the man who was walking up to the tower door. He was carrying an armful of boxes, which he put down on the ground before glancing around suspiciously, like a man who had something to hide. He then let himself into the tower with a large black key – gripping it in his left hand which, they could see through the telescope, had one finger missing...

"Edmund Groby," Ralph breathed.

Beth nodded. She'd know the sullen features of Vale's evil main henchman anywhere. He'd been involved in every plot against the King that they had foiled – and he was a terrifying adversary. A shudder of excitement went through her as she realized how close they were to catching their prey. Vale's gang *was* here, and for the first time, they had proof!

# Chapter Four

**Tread Lightly**

John had been keen to try and apprehend Groby the moment they'd first seen him, but Beth knew they had to gather more intelligence before alerting the enemy to their presence. Luckily they didn't have to wait long before the squat, dark figure showed himself again. The next day, while Ralph lay sprawled across the floor and John sat slumped in a chair – both of them asleep and snoring like drunkards – Beth saw Groby again. He peered out from behind the tower door and looked left and right. Once he had assured himself nobody was there, he slipped out. Without taking her eyes off him,

Beth made a note.

Then she froze.

There was another man coming out of the tower. Vale? Beth held her breath and watched closely. No. It wasn't Vale, but a man she knew nonetheless, though his face now bore hideous burn scars, and he walked with a pronounced limp.

"Ed Hewer?" she whispered to herself. "I … I thought he'd died in the Great Fire." Hewer had been a low-level henchmen and accomplice of Vale and Groby in the last attempt on the King's life. "John! Wake up, quick!"

"Huh?" John jerked awake, knocking over the cup beside him on the nightstand. He flung the blankets off his knees and scrambled over to Beth. "Is it Vale?"

"Look." She let him take the telescope and watched his expression change from curiosity to furious anger.

"Him!" John snarled. He clenched his fists. "As scarred as his soul, but that's Hewer all right. God, if there's any justice in the world I'll get to kill that man myself!"

Beth had expected this reaction from John as soon as she saw the man she thought had perished in the flames at Blackfriars church. Hewer had been involved in the plot to kidnap Polly, John's sister, who the villains had tried to use as blackmail to get John to help them.

Threatening his family was the one sure way to transform him from a kind, softly-spoken Navy Board clerk into a hard fighting man.

"Whatever's going on in that tower, it's big," Beth said. "Strange needs to know."

According to the terms of the mission, one of them was supposed to meet Strange at noon each day for a report, "unless the situation was urgent", in which case they could find him at the Corinthian Club. Short of discovering Vale himself in this bolthole, Beth couldn't think of a way this could be any more urgent. Vale's men were gathering – something important must be happening.

"I'll go," John said, stretching and trying to shake the sleep from his body.

"No." Beth laid a restraining hand on him. "You keep watch. I'll go and make the report."

Keeping out of sight, Beth slipped out of the cottage and made her way back into the City of London, hiring a boatman to take her down the Thames once she was safely away from the ruins of Richmond Palace. She managed to get Strange to come outside of his gentlemen's club by pretending she was a maid from his household with an urgent message. He quickly whisked Beth off to a side street as soon as he saw her, pulling on his cloak.

"You had better have a damn good reason for this visit," he hissed. "You're putting us both at risk by meeting me here, do you understand that?"

"Vale's men are at the tower," she told him, remaining calm and steady. "Groby and Hewer. We've seen both of them there – and once Groby was carrying boxes."

"Just those two?" Strange began to pace up and down.

"There may be more of them inside, we've seen lights moving around. But so far, only those two have left the building."

Strange looked at her. Although his face was expressionless, a spark of excitement was burning in his deep black eyes. "Then Vale himself may be within…"

"Ralph wants to get inside the tower," Beth told him. "He says we'll find out more that way."

"He's right," Strange said. "The time for surveillance is over. I appreciate it will be a difficult undertaking, but you must find a way to get inside. It sounds as though they are preparing for something. They may be getting ready to flee. I will not allow that."

*We must get inside*, Beth thought. *Easy for him to say…*

"We'll find a way in," she assured him. If anyone could, Ralph could.

 47

* * *

The moment Ralph heard the news he began firing off plans like a criminal mastermind.

"Front door's out, obviously," he began, his thoughts coming a mile a minute. "Far too exposed, and they'll be expecting it. If this had been some other gang of villains, I'd have said we dress up in disguise and try to fast-talk our way in, but this is Vale's lot, and they're not stupid. Besides, Groby will recognize us. All the windows on the ground floor look like stained glass, and that ain't the sort of window that opens, so we couldn't jemmy one…"

"Maybe there's a back door," Beth suggested. "We *have* only seen one side of the tower, yes?"

"We need to scout the place out," Ralph agreed. "It'll be dark soon. There's plenty of scrub around the outskirts. It'll hide us if we keep our heads down."

They took a few moments to gather what they needed. Ralph took a length of mooring rope, John a shuttered storm lantern that would give light if they absolutely had to have it. Beth took nothing but a hatpin, thinking it might be useful for picking locks. Ralph had shown her something of the art, but she was still learning. Besides, she thought, she could always use it as a weapon if there was any trouble.

Outside, the evening surprised them with its chill. A trace of mist had gathered, making the few remaining buildings look even more desolate.

Ralph grinned.

"That fog will make us even harder to see," he whispered. "Come on."

Bending low, keeping out of sight among the bushes and bracken, they made their way from the back of the boathouse to the edge of the palace grounds. Approaching from behind gave them their first good look at the place. There was no surrounding wall at the edge of the grounds as Beth had feared, just a ditch where the stones had been.

"Jump," said Ralph. "It's not wide."

Beth looked down. Dark, muddy water lay three feet below. As she watched, a rat jumped in with a plop and she grimaced, but then she steeled herself and jumped across to the other side. The mist was thicker now. She was standing in a broad field that had once been a courtyard, and heaps of broken stone lay here and there like burial mounds, waiting to be sold. *Those used to be pieces of the palace*, she thought. *Those were walls that kept the royal children safe. Now they're just rubble.*

49

"There's the tower," Ralph said. "And there's light. Someone's at home…"

"And there's our way in!" John said, pointing. "Look!"

Beth could see the roofless building adjoining the tower more clearly now. Judging from the shape of it, it had once been the palace chapel. The front wall had looked mostly intact from the boathouse, but she now saw the back had been torn away, revealing the wooden beams and joists.

"They haven't finished breaking it up yet," she whispered. "We can climb those stones easily. There's bound to be an inside door."

"Let's go." John set off at a run across the grass.

Ralph hissed, stopping him in his tracks. "Use them piles of stone for cover. Don't just dash out over the green like a startled rabbit!"

"Right. Sorry." John ducked behind one of the cairns. Together, they ran from pile to pile, moving closer to the ruined chapel.

A light went on in another of the upstairs rooms.

They all froze in place behind a cairn. Ralph held up a warning hand. Beth didn't even dare breathe. Slowly he peered out from behind the rocks, then gave them an *all clear* nod.

One last sprint and they were at the chapel wall. The wet grass had soaked Beth's shoes through and her stockings squelched. One after another they vaulted the remaining stones and stood in the gathering darkness.

Five minutes passed. The three spies knew that they had to wait, in order to be totally sure nobody had seen them. Nobody spoke. They glanced at each other's fearful faces, and then, after what felt like an hour, Ralph signalled for them to start exploring. Soon after, John made urgent come-and-see gestures – he'd found a door into the tower from the chapel.

Ralph mimed turning the handle very slowly, and John followed his lead. There was the tiniest of clunks from the latch and he leaned his weight against the door, but it didn't move. He mouthed the word *locked* to Ralph, who mouthed a word back that Beth pretended not to see.

There *had* to be a way in. She looked up. The bare roof beams lay above their heads like an exposed ribcage, open to the weather. The top of the tower was only a few feet higher. She tapped Ralph on the shoulder and pointed upwards. Ralph stared, broke into a grin and nodded. "Perfect! We can climb up there," he whispered. "If we shuffle across them roof beams, we can shinny up

to the top of the tower and let ourselves in!"

"Are you out of your mind?" John hissed. "One, those beams look like they're fit to collapse, and two, how are we meant to reach them?"

Ralph put his arm around John's shoulder. "See that wall, where the stone blocks have been pulled away? We can use it like a staircase."

"And jump the last three feet to the beam?"

"You jumped that ditch, didn't you?"

John's voice was like a bat's squeak: "That drop wouldn't have broken my neck if I'd missed it! And look at that last bit, where the beam runs up to the wall. We'd have to balance like ... like ... tightrope walkers!"

"So?" Ralph said with a shrug. "Scared?"

"I don't recall teasing you when you were quaking in your boots to go down the chimney of Somerset House!" John retorted. As part of their investigations into the kidnapping of John's sister, the three spies had found themselves in a tight spot not so long ago, and Ralph's fear of small spaces had made itself very clear.

"Very well," Ralph conceded, blushing. "Let's tie this rope around our waists. That way, if one of us slips, the others can keep them from falling. Satisfied?"

"Good plan," Beth interrupted. "Let's do it."

Ralph looped the stray piece of rope around each of them, knotting it securely and leaving a few feet of slack between each person. Then they began to climb.

Ralph – who had once served on board sea-going ships and was happy high in the air on a slim beam – led the way, with John in the middle and Beth following behind. The ruined wall that led up to the beam looked easy enough to climb. The stone blocks were wide and it *was* almost like a set of steps, Beth thought. But when she put her weight on a stone that looked secure, it shifted under her.

"Don't take a step without testing it first," Ralph warned. "Put your hands and feet where I do."

"Like Good King Wenceslas," John muttered.

They picked their way up the broken wall. Soon there was only a three-foot gap left before the clump of masonry where the beam jutted out. Ralph jumped over as if he were born to it and landed on the tiny platform. He immediately straddled the beam and shuffled forwards to make room for the others. John hesitated, but gathered himself and made the jump. He joined Ralph on the roof beam. Now there was only Beth.

"Don't look down," Ralph urged her.

Before she could stop herself, Beth looked. Suddenly

the stones seemed to sway and buckle beneath her. She clung tightly onto the final block, not having really registered how far it was to fall. The rubble-strewn chapel floor looked as distant as the sea at the bottom of a cliff.

"Just jump!" Ralph's voice came to her. "You have to do it now or you never will!"

Beth stood up shakily, braced herself … and jumped. The stone platform accepted her weight, and Ralph gave a little cheer. "See? Nothing to it!"

Beth closed her eyes. The sound of her heart hammering drowned out everything else, and she sat for a while, calming down before opening them again.

"Let's keep going."

John smiled and reached out to pat her on the shoulder. "I'm proud of you, Beth—"

Just then, a crucial piece of masonry somewhere came loose. Stones rattled, and the beam dropped half a foot and tilted sideways. John tipped over and fell off, screaming before they could warn him about the noise.

"Brace!" Ralph hissed. Beth and Ralph grabbed the beam with both arms just as the rope went taut, catching John's full weight. The force knocked the wind out of her but she held on tight. For an instant Beth was sure she'd see John's broken body far below on the floor. But he was

dangling in mid-air, gasping from the rope biting into his waist, flailing his arms and legs. She gripped hard with her thighs and leaned down as far as she dared.

"Take my hand!"

John made panicky, gasping noises as he reached out and grabbed for Beth's hand. Their fingers brushed, and she stretched an agonizing few inches more, knowing that if she fell, Ralph couldn't possibly hold them both…

But John's next lunge clasped her hand and held it tight. Steadily, a little at a time, she and Ralph pulled him back up to the beam.

"Good to have you back with us," Ralph said, gasping for breath. "Try not to do that again, all right?"

From that moment on they sacrificed speed for safety. They steadily made their way over the beams, pausing every time they heard the creak of wood or the crunch of sliding stone. Beth had the sickening feeling John's scream had to have been heard from inside the tower. They could easily be going through all of this only to find themselves captured, or worse.

Ralph finally reached the far end of the beam and pulled himself up through the ruined roof. "I can reach the battlements, easy," he whispered. "There's a trap door up here – just pray it's unlocked!"

Only once they were all standing safely at the top of the tower, with the rope unfastened and put away, did Ralph try the trap door. It lifted easily, and they could see dusty stone steps leading down into darkness.

Ralph licked his dry lips.

"We're in."

# Chapter Five

## Into the Tower

Treading softly, still speaking only in whispers and hand gestures, they descended the stairs into a large, darkened chamber. The tall windows in the walls let in only the faintest scraps of light from the dying day outside. Five or six large objects stood in the centre of the room, and two more sets of steps led further down into the tower.

Beth crossed to the window and looked out. The river glimmered in the faint moonlight and willows dangled their tendrils in the water like humpbacked figures.

"This place used to be a prison cell," John said, pointing out iron rings in the wall that had chains hanging from

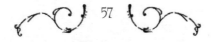

them. "Why would you need a prison in a palace?"

"Keep your friends close and your enemies closer?" Ralph guessed. "Anyway, look at the rust. Nobody's been locked up here in years. Let's have a look around."

The new owner – Beth was convinced she knew who it was – was using the place as a combined storeroom and office. The objects piled up in the centre of the room proved to be travelling trunks, and a writing desk stood in the corner. She caught her breath as she saw how neatly the quill, ink, papers and sand had been laid out. Whoever had done that was a careful, meticulous planner. Beth's stomach churned with excitement.

"This trunk's open," John hissed.

Beth tore herself away from the desk and went to look. It was full of clothes. Like the desk, everything was neat – carefully folded and stacked. There were many different garments, almost like the wardrobe department of her theatre. Beth fingered the cloth, taking note of the quality. Then something else struck her.

"This is a gentleman's coat. But this is a clergyman's shirt, do you see? And this is a military jacket, ribbons and all."

"Why are they bringing clothes for half a dozen different men?" Ralph muttered.

"They aren't," said Beth meaningfully. She held up two of the shirts so that Ralph could see the sizes matched exactly. "These are all for one man."

Ralph's mouth opened as he suddenly understood what Beth meant. "No wonder they've never caught him. He's thought of everything, ain't he?"

Beth's gaze fell on a pile of white silk kerchiefs. They were of exceptional quality, the finest money could buy. The sort of thing a man couldn't bear to part with, even if he'd had to leave all else behind…

"Almost everything," she whispered. She gently picked up one of the kerchiefs. It was as light and fine as gossamer. And there, in the corner, was the embroidered mark she'd been looking for: HJV.

*Henry J. Vale.*

"It's him," she said softly. "Look."

John frowned. "He goes to all that trouble to hide his identity, then has his kerchiefs monogrammed? Maybe he's not as smart as we thought."

"No, he's had these for a long time," Beth said. She could feel it with her deepest instincts. "These are souvenirs of who he used to be, back when he had power and wealth. He must have taken them with him when he fled the country."

From the floor below came the sound of a door closing.

"Listen!" John hissed.

They all fell silent.

Next moment, footsteps were coming up the stairs. More than one person.

"Hide!"

Ralph and John dashed across the room to the staircase that led up to the top of tower and hunkered down in the dark, hoping whoever was coming had no reason to go up that far. Beth ran the other way, to the window. She hid behind the curtain, feeling half terrified and half ridiculous. What a childish hiding place – and yet there was no time to change her mind. Were her feet sticking out? She had no way to know. Very carefully she put one eye to the tiny gap between the curtains.

Two men came into the room, one of them holding a lamp that blazed like a bonfire in her dark-accustomed eyes. Even through the dazzle, she could see it was Hewer – and she could hear his raspy breathing, a result of the smoke from the Great Fire, she guessed. For a moment she let herself imagine a desperate swordfight with Hewer on top of the tower, ending with her kicking the man off the edge. Then she shook her head quickly.

That was the stuff of stage melodrama. This was reality.

"What's to be done with this lot?" said the other man, the one Beth didn't recognize. He had a large wart on his neck that dangled repulsively like a turkey's wattle.

"The other stuff's already gone – to *Dorcas*," said Hewer. He sighed, coughing a little as he did. "On second thoughts let's leave these where they are for now. They can go with himself in the carriage tonight."

*Dorcas?* Beth thought.

The man nodded. "Anything to bring from up top?"

Beth held her breath as the men looked in John and Ralph's direction.

"No," Hewer said. "Nobody ever goes up there except him, and he only does it when he wants to have a quiet think. Walking the battlements, like. Come on. We've time for a beer before we start."

As the two of them left the room, Beth slipped out of hiding. "They're gone," she whispered up to the others.

John stood up and emerged from the shadows. "Thank God."

"They'll be back," Ralph said. "You two search the place, fast. I'll keep lookout."

Beth nodded, and began quickly looking through the writing desk in the corner. Oddly, the drawer contained

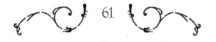

61

bills of sale for large amounts of tobacco, all organized by date. There was a sheaf of paperwork relating to shipping too. The writer – Vale beyond a doubt – had been sending cargoes backwards and forwards to America.

"John, look at this!"

"So that's how he's making his money," John said. "Trading with the New World."

"Hurry it up!" Ralph whispered.

"Who do you suppose Dorcas could be?" Beth asked, leafing quickly through the papers.

"Perhaps a housekeeper in Vale's new house?" guessed John. "Or maybe Vale has a daughter none of us know about?"

Now there was a possibility Beth didn't want to dwell upon. Vale had many lives now. That gave her a thought. "Every one of these costumes is one of Vale's identities. We need to try and take note of all of them. It could be a big help in tracking him down if he got away…"

Ralph nodded. "You check the outfits and anything else that's in the trunks. I'll go with John and see what we can search of the rest of the tower."

"Be careful," John warned.

"Be quick!" Beth replied. The young men headed off down the front stairs.

Left alone, Beth began rifling through the trunks as fast as she could. Every time she came across a new kind of outfit, she made a note. Vale had thought of everything, she realized; even his henchmen had multiple sets of clothes, so that they could blend in without arousing suspicion.

"But you're not as cunning as you like to think you are, Mister Vale," she whispered. "There's always someone out there who's cleverer than you. Someone you'll never expect."

After five minutes of rummaging she had noted down seven of Vale's separate identities. She kneeled down with her back to the rear stairs to start work on a new trunkload, but this one was mostly filled only with silken bedsheets and pillowcases. There had to be more interesting stuff buried deeper down. She eagerly pulled the sheets out, leaving them piling up on the floor next to her, but there seemed to be nothing inside but an endless supply of bedding. Beth leaned in to check for a false bottom, absolutely certain she would find one. She was so engrossed that she never heard anyone come into the room.

She only knew the man behind her was there when he spoke.

"Oi! Who are you? What are you up to?"

Beth tried to turn around, but he was on her too fast, and she realized it was the man with the hideous wart who had been in here before. He had her wrists in his grasp before she could do anything. She tried to kick his shins and twist her arms free, but he held her at arm's length, pushing her painfully back over the lip of the trunk. An ugly grin spread over his face and he pushed harder, forcing her all the way inside.

"No!" Beth yelled. "Don't!"

He gave a final brutal shove, forcing her down into the depths of the trunk, then slammed the lid. She tried to straighten up, forcing her shoulders against the lid like Atlas supporting the world, but the man had his weight on the trunk lid now and she couldn't budge it. The lock gave a sharp rattle and click and she heard the key being taken out. Then his footsteps moved away.

*I'm trapped in here*, she thought. *He's locked it.*

She was too furious with herself to panic. Being caught with her back to an entrance? That was an amateur error. Never mind what Strange would think – *she* was bitterly angry. She ought to be better than that by now.

The chest was uncomfortable, cramped and pitch dark, and the smell of lavender was overpowering.

*To keep moths away*, she thought. Now panic began to set in, welling up under the anger. She really was trapped in here and she could do nothing about it. She could smash her hands and feet against the wood until they were bloody, and it would do no good.

*Think*, she told herself. *You need to breathe. So how are you going to?* The keyhole! Wart-man had removed the key. She set her lips against the cold metal and inhaled, sucking air into her lungs. It was hard going, but it was enough. She forced herself to calm down and control her breathing. If she could take slow breaths, she'd not only have a better chance of surviving, she'd keep the panic at bay too.

There were voices outside. Beth pushed her ear against the keyhole to listen.

"...still in there, is she?" said Hewer's raspy voice.

"Well, I didn't know what else to do wiv 'er, did I?" said the wart-man. "I came in 'ere and she was pinching the sheets..."

"She wasn't," Hewer said scornfully. "She was looking for something. Odds on she's a spy."

"What do we do, then? Kill her?"

Beth's heart pounded. She drew her hatpin out. She might get one chance, if she was lucky. She'd

aim for the eyes.

"Not without himself's say-so," Hewer said. "He doesn't want any killing done unless he's given the word personally. Besides, he'll want to know she was poking around."

"You'd better tell him, then."

"Of course I'll tell him, you coward. But now she's in there, we best not let her out. You drag the trunk down the back stairs to Vale's study. Let me do the talking."

Panic hit Beth then like a cannonball in the stomach. She was trapped, about to be hauled into the presence of Henry Vale himself. He was a killer – he'd done it countless times before. And she knew, with a sickening deep-down certainty, that he wouldn't kill her quickly and cleanly. Not Vale. He must know she was Strange's agent, so he'd want to make her talk first. Milk her for every last agonizing drop of information. She would probably *wish* she was dead before he was done with her. And now the trunk was moving.

She was being pulled across the floor.

# Chapter Six

**In His Presence**

"I wish we could have brought a lantern with us," John whispered as he and Ralph descended the stairs. "Or even a candle. It's so dark in this place. I expect Vale likes it that way."

"Carrying a light's the easiest way to get yourself noticed," Ralph replied, then he grunted in pain as he hit his shin on a wooden crate, all but invisible in the near darkness.

"I know!" John hissed. "But how are we meant to look for clues if we can't *see* anything?"

"I've flint and tinder. How about we shut up, eh?"

They groped their way to the foot of the stairs and found themselves in a passage with doors on all sides. The sound of gruff voices came from behind the door at the end. It was slightly ajar, and light flickered in the narrow gap. John was about to suggest they turn round, but Ralph was already heading forward. The voices grew louder. Six men, maybe more. John swallowed. They were more heavily outnumbered than he'd expected.

"This lot must have been in here all along," whispered Ralph. "Hewer and Groby must have brought them food and drink from outside. That'll be what the boxes were. Supplies."

"Who are they?"

"Vale's personal bodyguards, at a guess," Ralph said quietly.

John glanced back down the passage, all but certain that someone would come down the stairs behind them at any moment. They'd be trapped if that happened. All of a sudden, it seemed like a very bad idea to still be here. They shouldn't have split up. Strange would have called that an amateur mistake…

"Let's fetch Beth and get out of here," he whispered.

"Hush up, can't you? I'm listening!"

John had no choice but to listen too.

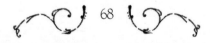

"…nothing left to do but wait," a man was saying. "When's that blasted carriage getting here?"

"Nine o'clock sharp," said another. "It won't be here a minute earlier or later. You know Vale. Everything has to be exact."

"God forbid you so much as crease his bedsheets," said another.

That remark made John think of the Dorcas person they'd mentioned. He doubted she was in there with the men, whoever she was. If she was staying at the tower, then maybe one of these rooms down the passageway belonged to her.

"Let's keep searching," he suggested. "We can't get inside that room to look around, can we? So let's check these others."

"Fair enough," Ralph finally agreed. They moved back down the hall, Ralph trying the doors, John watching out for approaching guards. Nothing stirred. John hoped Beth was all right where she was.

The first two doors were locked, but the third opened onto a pitch-black room. They quickly ducked inside and Ralph sparked a light. The tiny flame revealed the furnishings of a bedchamber. The bed was an ornate four-poster, but the curtains and bedding had been

removed, leaving only a mattress. A wooden wig stand stood on a dresser.

"Vale's room," Ralph said. "Who else out of this lot would wear a wig, eh?"

"Looks like he's cleaned the place out," John said. He pulled open the drawers, revealing them to be empty. "Why would he … Hang on. It's obvious. They're getting ready to abandon this place for good!"

"You're right! Vale's not just getting ready for another mission. He's jumping ship!"

"And the carriage arrives here at nine, they said. There's just enough time to tell Strange what's going on. We've got to go and get Beth—"

But they both froze as he said this. Footsteps were approaching fast.

Ralph blew the flame out. "Under the bed!" he whispered.

They scrambled into the tiny space under the slats and lay there, praying that the door wouldn't open.

"Lads!" a voice was calling. John clenched his fists. *Hewer!* "Listen to this. You'll never believe what Mathers has gone and done!"

A babble of answering voices: "What?" "Go on, then." "What's he done now?"

"He's only gone and caught a spy!"

John felt as if he were falling through the tower floor. It had to be Beth. Beside him he heard Ralph whisper, "Oh no. Oh no."

"Get away," one of the men said lazily.

"It's the truth! Mathers caught her going through Vale's things. He's holding her prisoner right now." The man gave a gloating chuckle. "Tell you what, I wouldn't want to be in her shoes when Vale gets done with her."

*Say where she is*, John thought fiercely. *Tell them where you're keeping her.*

"So," said one of the guards, "do we get to watch?"

"Mathers is taking her to Vale," Hewer replied, sounding disappointed. "I'm going back up there now. But you've all got your orders and you're to wait for the carriage like we were told."

"Don't worry about missing the show," said a different bodyguard. "Most likely you'll be able to hear the screams!"

The men all laughed, and Ralph and John said nothing to one another. They didn't need to. Silently they slipped out of their hiding place, opened the door, and headed for the staircase.

\* \* \*

The trunk jolted every time it bumped down a step, but Beth refused to make a sound. She didn't want to give whoever was out there the satisfaction. Besides, if she stayed quiet for long enough, they might think she was running out of air and open the trunk to let her breathe.

She was a captive spy. That made her valuable – too valuable to kill without questioning first. The thought of her coming interrogation ran cold fingers of dread down her spine, but at least it meant Vale would keep her alive to do so, and that bought her time; hopefully, enough time for Ralph and John to come and find her. If only she hadn't had her stupid back to those stupid stairs! She wanted to kick herself, but there was no way to do it in this cramped space.

After more painful bumping down stairs, the trunk came to a stop. A new voice was speaking now, one Beth hadn't heard before. Ear to the keyhole, she strained to hear what he was saying.

"…believe I left strict instructions that I was not to be disturbed?"

"Yes, sir, I'm sorry, sir, but under the circumstances I thought you'd want to know," said Hewer. He sounded

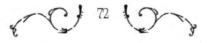

like a grovelling butler instead of the thug he was.

"I'm busy. Get out."

"B-but we're under standing orders to tell you if we catch spies, Mister Vale," Hewer whined, his dry voice cracking.

Finally she was in Vale's presence, Beth thought. His was a cultured voice, soft, very precise, and her life depended on what it said next. Beth stayed perfectly still, listening. Vale sighed wearily, and Beth heard a drawer slide shut.

"Go on."

"It was Mathers who found her, sir, not me," said Hewer. "He found a strange girl rooting through the trunks in the room upstairs, didn't you?"

Mathers mumbled an affirmative.

"A girl?"

"Yes, sir," Hewer replied. "He shoved her in the trunk, so as to keep her from escaping, and we thought we'd best let you know right away, sir."

"And the contents of the trunk? Did you attend to them?"

Silence for a moment. Then: "Mathers left them on the floor."

"I see," said Vale. "My personal effects are left lying in

the dirt. Attend to the matter now, Mathers, or I will be most displeased."

Beth heard Mathers hurry out of the room. A chair slid back. She heard Vale pat his hand on the top of the trunk. A mere thickness of wood divided her from him now. She could feel his presence through the lid of the chest.

"Well done," he said quietly.

Beth wasn't sure for a moment whether he was talking to her or to Hewer. Was this some strange token of respect?

"Thank you, sir," Hewer said.

"I'm not at all surprised to find one of the King's running dogs sniffing at my trail," Vale said. "A mangy pack of them seems to shadow my every step. Do you know what is odd, though, Hewer?"

"Sir?"

"This is the first time they've sent a little *girl*." Vale laughed. The sound wasn't at all pleasant. Beth thought of cold steel scissors snipping.

"Do you want to see her, sir?"

Beth braced herself. Despite the fear coursing through her, she gripped the hatpin tightly like a dagger. When the lid opened, she would strike. This was her chance to

end the threat of Vale once and for all.

"Why would I want to do that?" Vale said smoothly.

Hewer blustered: "I thought you might want to, um, interrogate her or something. Find out what she knows, like."

"Alas, we are short on time, and a proper interrogation cannot be rushed," Vale said. "It takes a certain ... *artistry* ... to wring the secrets out of a spy. Brute force alone will not do."

"So what should I do with her, then?"

"Best dispose of her. I doubt she knows anything of use, in any case."

"Yes, sir." Hewer began to do as he was bid, but then he paused. "Dispose of her ... how?"

"Come now," said Vale impatiently. "You were a boy once. You know what to do with unwanted puppies, surely?"

"D-drown 'em?"

"There is a deep river right opposite us," Vale pointed out, like a teacher explaining something to an exceptionally stupid pupil. "I think that trunk might accidentally fall into it, don't you?"

Hewer chuckled nervously. "Oh ... as you wish, Mister Vale."

Beth felt the trunk begin to move again, and she shivered in horror. There was no way out of this prison. If it fell into the river, it – and her lungs – would fill with water in minutes. She would drown, just like a puppy in a weighted sack. *I'm not too valuable to kill at all*, she thought. *Vale didn't even want to see me. He's having me killed without a second thought!*

# Chapter Seven

**Below the Surface**

"We've got one hour until the carriage arrives," John told Ralph. "When it does, Vale's cronies will be running all over this place, fetching his things and making sure he gets away safely. We have to find Beth before then."

"That upstairs room used to be a prison cell," Ralph whispered. "Let's start there."

They dashed to the end of the corridor and up the stairs. John braced himself for a fight. The one thing in their favour was surprise. He could strike from the darkness, maybe drop one of Vale's men before they realized who was attacking them...

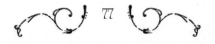

But the storeroom was dark and silent as before. Beth was not hanging from the ancient manacles in the wall. Something was different, though. John couldn't put his finger on what it was.

"Back stairs," Ralph ordered.

They spent the next ten minutes frantically searching, ducking in and out of rooms and hiding around corners. There was no sign of Beth anywhere.

Suddenly Ralph pulled John inside a stinking room that had clearly been used as a garbage dump, as Hewer rounded a corner.

"Talk to me like that," he muttered as he went past them with his limping gait. "Thinks he can order me about like one of his lackeys … and … and *dispose* of a girl…?"

They peered around the door as Hewer retreated into the dark.

"I could knock him down," Ralph whispered. "Then we could *make* him tell us where Beth is?"

"We can't risk it. If he shouted out, this place would be down on us like a pack of wolves!"

"I wouldn't give him the chance to shout," Ralph said, grim-faced. "I've had practice. Come on. Let's crack his skull."

The thought of coshing Hewer over the head was sweet, but John still refused. "We're gambling with Beth's life! We have to find out where they've taken her, and fast. We can't risk being captured too, then what would we do?"

"All right, all right!" Ralph ran his hand through his unruly hair and frowned hard. "If Vale's leaving at nine, he's going to want to take her with him, isn't he?"

"That makes sense. Let's follow Hewer – maybe he'll lead us to her. They'll be waiting to load her up with all the other stuff. He'll whisk her off in his carriage when he goes to meet with Dorcas."

They snuck quickly back up to the uppermost room after Hewer and crouched, hiding in the shadows once again as a group of men came into the room carrying lanterns. They began to lift the trunks and carry them down, grumbling and cursing as they did so. *They're getting ready for the carriage*, John thought. *Vale wants everything primed to go without delay.*

"What about that other trunk?" one of the men said. "Could have sworn there was one more."

"You just forget you ever saw it," another, husky voice said nastily. Hewer.

"Yeah, Hewer here is taking care of loading that one,"

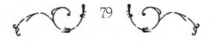

added yet another, with a laugh.

"Do you think … it sounds like they've got Beth in a *trunk*!" Ralph whispered urgently.

"I think you're right," John whispered back, his heart sinking.

"We have to get out of here."

"And leave Beth behind?" John struggled to keep his voice hushed. "You heard what they said. You know what they'll do to her!"

"Look, mate, I'm not chuffed about it either, but we've not got a choice! We need to think of a plan."

"We could fight!"

"Not against that many. Hang on. You remember what that crate looked like, don't you? We could wait until the carriage arrives and they lug it out to the forecourt, then we go and bust it open, and we all run like merry hell."

"It's not a great plan," John said. His flesh was still crawling at the thought of leaving Beth in the hands of these brutes. "But it's the only one we've got. Let's do it—"

"Hey!" said one of the men shifting the trunks. "Did you hear that?"

John and Ralph pressed their backs against the wall. Someone was coming their way.

"Hear what?" Hewer replied warily.

"I could have sworn I heard someone talking just then." There was a long pause, and then the man shrugged. The light retreated. "Must have been one of the others. Or," he paused dramatically, "this place *is* haunted, you know. Stands to reason, doesn't it? Tear down a palace, and there's bound to be some restless spirits wandering around. And you know what they used to use this place for, don't you?" The man rattled one of the chains hanging from the wall.

"You know your problem? You've got an overactive imagination."

"Oh yeah?"

"Well, I'm not the one hearing voices, am I?"

Still arguing, the two men heaved their trunk down the stairs and away. John let out a long breath, but his relief didn't last long. There was no way they could escape through any of the exits on the ground floor. They'd have to contend with the horror of the derelict chapel again.

John and Ralph swiftly made their way back up and over the battlements, then lowered themselves down to the crossbeam. A wind was picking up, and it made John's bones ache with cold. He wasn't sure he had the energy for another climb, much less the nerve.

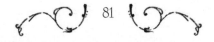

But he had to. Beth needed him.

"Don't worry," Ralph grinned. "Getting down's always easier than getting up. Quicker too." With that, he tied the rope around the beam and went scrambling down it like a monkey, dropping the last few feet to the ground below.

John followed. The rope burned his hands and his grip was weakening, but he managed it. "I don't think anyone saw," he gasped. "But what if they find the rope?"

"We'll just have to chance it. Come on!"

Together they ran across the cairn-studded field at the back of the tower and crouched among the bushes. John rubbed his sore hands together to get some warmth back into them. Now there was nothing to do but wait.

The carriage arrived promptly at nine. No sooner had the wheels come to a standstill than Vale's men came hurrying out of the tower. The trunks emerged one by one. John counted them as the men loaded them onto the carriage.

"I only count four," he whispered to Ralph. "There's still one missing."

"Give it a moment longer," Ralph murmured. "Come on, Beth! Where are you?"

John's legs were aching, both from squatting down in

the cold for so long and from the tension. People were milling around in the courtyard now and he could hear raised voices, but there was no sign of Beth.

"Maybe they're not keeping her in one of the trunks," he guessed. "Or she's still in the tower somewhere. What are we going to do?"

"I don't know!" Ralph snarled. "Just keep watching, damn it. And keep your mouth shut – one of them might say something."

John strained to hear. He caught a word that might have been "Dorcas" and another that sounded like "sail" but might have been "Vale", or "fail" for all he knew. The horses were stamping their hooves restlessly and the driver seemed impatient to get going.

John made up his mind not to let that carriage out of his sight, even if he had to run across the courtyard and leap onto it. *Stay safe, Beth, wherever you are*, he thought. *We're coming to get you, no matter what it takes…*

Beth's trunk was moving again. Whoever was carrying it clearly didn't care for her comfort; her head was repeatedly bashed against the side as she jolted down

the stairs. They were probably enjoying it, she reflected ruefully. They must like thinking of her all pummelled and bruised like a loose apple in a barrel. At least they'd stopped short of kicking her down the stairs – so far. A vicious tooth-rattling whack made her eyes water. That settled it. They were doing this on purpose. Beth kept a tight grip on her long pin. Even if she couldn't use it as a weapon, she might be able to get the trunk open with it. *All I need*, she told herself, *is for this trunk to stop moving for a few moments before they drop me in the water. If I can get the lock open, I can open the lid underwater and they'll never know I haven't drowned.*

But a nasty voice at the back of her mind whispered: *The Thames is freezing. What if you fumble? What if the lock won't open? All that dirty cold water flooding into the trunk, soaking your clothes, rushing into your lungs, choking off your last bubbling breath…*

"Shut up," she whispered to herself. She felt the trunk being set down. On grass, by the sound of it, not gravel. Water was gurgling somewhere nearby – she had to be on the bank of the Thames. The men who were carrying her must have stopped for a breather before throwing her in. That meant she had a chance. Ignoring the pain in her head, she set to work with the pin, scraping it

84

around inside the lock, trying to catch the crucial little tag of metal.

"Listen to that," growled Hewer from outside. "Puppy's scratching."

There was a violent thump. Next second, Beth fell back heavily. After a moment's confusion, she realized the trunk had been tipped over. They weren't bothering to carry her to the water's edge – they were just rolling her down! Where was the pin? She scrambled for it, but she couldn't find it anywhere, and the lock hadn't budged even the tiniest fraction of an inch. The trunk flipped over again, leaving Beth upside down inside. Now she was really beginning to panic. In seconds, she'd be drowning, with no way out.

*No*, she told herself. *John and Ralph wouldn't let that happen. Vale's men can't have caught them, or I'd have heard them talking, wouldn't I? They must be out there, waiting to come and rescue me. Please, Lord, let them be out there!*

She heard Groby say, "Come on. We've had our fun. Get it over with, Hewer."

Then she was tumbling like a drowning mariner sucked into a whirlpool. Jolt after painful jolt slammed into her body. Rage took over and she lashed out angrily, kicking the trunk lid. It couldn't be that strong, could

it? She'd just have to smash her way out. But it did no good. She collapsed, exhausted, as the first splash of water broke over the trunk…

Ralph and John caught the briefest of glimpses of Vale as he strode from the tower towards the carriage – a tall, lean, dark figure, his face mostly hidden by a scarf. The driver cracked his whip and the carriage lurched away, picking up speed as it went.

"What if Beth's in there?" John hissed. "We have to get after the carriage and—"

Just then, from the other side of the building, there was a mighty splash. John and Ralph shared a horrified glance.

"They've thrown her in!" John burst out.

"Come on." Ralph was already up and running.

But if John hadn't heard Hewer and Groby talking as they came around the corner, they would have run smack into them. As it was, John had just enough time to grab Ralph and dive back into cover behind a mound of fallen masonry. Groby was wearing a nasty smirk.

"Vale was right, you know," he said. "It *is* just like

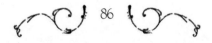

drowning puppies in a sack."

"What if someone finds her?" Hewer fretted. "If anyone discovers what we've just done, they'd hang us!"

"They won't find her. She's sunk deep and that trunk's heavy. Even when she rots and puffs up, she'll stay down."

"You've done this before, haven't you?" Hewer said shakily.

Together, their hard work done for now, the two men strolled back to the tower.

The moment they were out of sight, John sprinted to the muddy river bank. Dying ripples were still washing against the shore. *Beth's down there*, he thought desperately.

Ralph pointed. Bubbles were breaking the surface. "Over there!"

"She'll drown!" John said. He and Ralph waded in after the sinking trunk. The bank sloped down steeply, and within seconds they were up to their waists in water. Frantically they ducked down beneath the surface, trying to find where Beth's trunk had ended up. Silt and weeds swirled around them. It was black and bitterly cold.

John came up for air and tried to see where the bubbles were coming from. A feeble flurry broke the surface only feet away. Encouraged, he dived down again and this

time his groping hand felt smooth wood. Quickly he surfaced again.

"Here! I've found her!" he hissed. Ralph swam over to him and together they duck-dived to reach the chest.

It was already waterlogged. Tugging at it wasn't enough – it wouldn't move. The weight of the chest and the water already inside it was too much. *We're going to lose her*, John thought. *She's drowning and she's only feet away from us. Unless they already killed her and this was their way of getting rid of the body…*

Panic making him unable to hold his breath any longer, he burst out of the water again. Ralph had been under the water for nearly a minute now, and just as John was fearing for his life too, he came to the surface with a spluttering gasp.

"Grab this and pull!"

Ralph proffered a sodden rope. "I tied it to the 'andle," he gasped. "Haul, for God's sake."

They backed up onto the shore, their feet squelching deep in the mud, and began to pull on the rope like sailors hauling up a mainsail. Slowly the dark shape of the trunk reappeared from the waters, inching up out of the river and back onto land.

Not a sound came from inside.

# Chapter Eight
**Fly by Night**

John tugged at the lid, but it wouldn't budge. "It's locked!"

"Of course it's ruddy locked," Ralph snapped. "She'd have got out otherwise, wouldn't she?"

From his pocket he drew a short metal pry-bar. He wiggled the flat end into the tiny crevice between the trunk's lid and its side. With a grunt of effort, he heaved at it. There was a splintery creak as something began to give, but the lid stayed shut. John looked on, feeling helpless to do anything. How much time had passed between the first splash and their hauling the trunk up out of

the water? At least five minutes. Probably more. The air wouldn't all rush out at once, he thought. She must have had some air to breathe. But then he remembered she'd been in there for ages, since she was first captured. For all he knew, she'd run out of air a long time ago…

As if he was trapped in a nightmare, John saw the sequence of events clearly. Ralph would crack open the lid and fling it back. There would be Beth, pale and staring-eyed, floating in her muddy coffin. Too late.

He shook his head and tried to focus on reality, but the image of Beth's dead, staring eyes wouldn't go away.

"Give us a hand," Ralph said urgently. "Can't shift the blasted thing."

John laid his hands over Ralph's and together they forced the pry-bar down. There was a groan and a crack, and then the whole lock section came free, ripped out of the wood like a tooth, still fastened to the lower part. The trunk lid fell with a hollow boom.

Beth lay there, curled up in a trunk full of water like some strange river spirit woken from a long winter hibernation. She was deathly white, and they stared for what felt like an eternity as she didn't seem to move. Then, suddenly, Beth drew a deep, shuddering breath, and began to cough.

She was alive!

John threw his arms around her and lifted her out of the trunk. She was soaking wet and freezing cold, but he didn't care.

"You're all right!" he laughed, burying his face in her wet hair. "I thought we'd lost you!"

Beth broke free from his embrace, just in time to burst out coughing once again. "I … I think I swallowed some of the river," she gasped.

"You're not a real Londoner until you've had a mouthful of the Thames," Ralph grinned.

"But how…" John couldn't get the words out. "How did you…?"

"How did I stay alive?" Beth said shakily. "My acting training helped…"

John stared. "Let me guess. You practised for the part of Ophelia in *Hamlet* by drowning yourself every day until you got used to it?"

Beth was breathing more easily now, and reached up to wring the cold, muddy water from her hair. "Of course … not!" she panted. "I mean breath control, that's all." Seeing John and Ralph looking blank, she explained, "All actors need to master their breathing, for projection and stamina." She coughed a little again, shivering.

"You've heard some of the speeches they make us recite, haven't you? Those things are *long*."

"So you just held your breath?" said Ralph.

"I slowed my breathing down until the trunk had completely filled up with water. *Then* I held my breath, for as long as I could, at least. Thank goodness you got me out in time…" She looked up at the tower, suddenly alert. "So what happened? Did you see where they went? Where's Vale?"

"He's gone," John said.

Beth's face fell. "We need to get after him!" She started to run, then staggered to a halt and coughed up another load of Thames water. "Can't … let him escape." She fell to her knees.

"Oh, no you don't!" John gently lifted Beth back to her feet. She gave him a bleary smile of thanks. "I don't think you're in any condition to go chasing off after anyone," he said.

Beth blew out her cheeks. "I'm as strong as an ox!"

Ralph and John looked at one another.

"Nice try," Ralph said.

Beth sighed. "I don't suppose we'd catch up with Vale's carriage anyway." She looked upriver towards the lights of central London. "We need to work out where

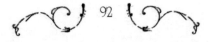

92

he's gone, though. Strange will skin us alive if he hears we let Vale get away."

"Most of his men left with him," John pointed out. "We should head back inside the tower now it's a bit safer to sneak around. See what we can find out."

"Good idea." Beth started towards the tower, but Ralph stopped her with a firm restraining arm.

"You aren't coming," he said. "You need to go home and get some rest."

Beth swatted feebly at Ralph. "Get off me!" She broke into a fresh burst of coughing.

"Listen to yourself," Ralph said quietly, but with gentle persistence. "You've water in your lungs. How are you going to sneak about in there if you can't go two minutes without coughing or sneezing, eh? Someone will hear."

Beth glared at him sullenly. "I'll just go back to the cottage and make us all some toasted muffins like a good little housemaid, then, shall I?"

"Go back to your lodgings and go to bed, for God's sake," Ralph insisted. "It's freezing out here and you're soaked through!"

"You're lucky to be alive, Beth," John said. "Ralph's right. You should rest."

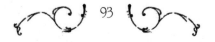

Now that she wasn't fighting for her life, Beth *was* suddenly feeling cold and tired. Maybe she *had* done enough for one night. She trusted them to do the rest of the job well.

"I'll be at the Peacock and Pie, then," she told them grudgingly. "Only 'til I get my strength back, though."

Not long after, Beth had set off in the cottage's little rowboat, while Ralph and John were making their way back into the tower. It was a lot easier to get in now that Ralph's rope was already hanging from the beam. Nobody was waiting inside the uppermost room, and all the chests had gone. Cautiously, moving with their backs to the wall, John and Ralph began their search.

It quickly became apparent that only two guards had been left in the building, and they were helping themselves to what was left of the food – and clearly drink, judging from their increasing sloppiness and loud voices. John was sure that Vale really had abandoned this roost, leaving only a skeleton crew behind in case something went wrong.

But where was he heading to now? A place like this

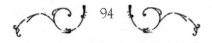

was perfect for a criminal like him to hide out in. It was secure, outside the city, and – as they'd discovered – not easy to see inside. So why abandon it?

Opposite the main bedroom lay an office they hadn't had the chance to explore before. By the light of an oil lamp, John leafed through papers while Ralph stood watch by the door.

"Found anything?"

"It's mostly shipping records," John murmured. "Cargoes of this and that, back and forth to America. He's dealing in tobacco and sugar. And slaves."

"Is that so," Ralph said. "What a lovely bloke."

"There's just too much stuff here. We could search for hours and not find anything but— Wait!"

John triumphantly held up an insignificant-looking scrap of paper. "We've got him, Ralph. It was staring us in the face. I can't believe I didn't think of this before."

"Think of what?"

"*Dorcas.* She's not a person at all. She's a ship!"

John's finger traced the words on the shipping invoice he'd found. The trunks they'd seen upstairs had been booked onto a ship called the *Dorcas.* By the look of it, Vale had paid extra to take such a huge amount of luggage with him.

95

"Maybe he's not just quitting this tower," Ralph said. "Maybe he's quitting the whole country. Start all over again in a foreign land, like."

John pocketed the invoice. "We find that ship and we find him. That name ring any bells?"

"Not to me," Ralph admitted. "Let's get out of here, eh? We've got what we came for."

John's heart pounded as they made their way back up the stairs. Everything now depended upon their reaching Strange with this information. He was sure he'd find the rope cut, or guards waiting to ambush them. The name *Dorcas* kept going around and around in his mind. He racked his brains to try and remember if he'd ever seen the ship before, but came up with nothing but a maddening blank.

Despite his fears, they made it back out of the tower without anyone trying to stop them. But as they reached the bank of the river and began the journey back, John stopped in his tracks.

"Look at the river, Ralph. The tide's going out."

"So?"

"Nobody with half a brain tries to navigate the Thames at low tide, do they? If Vale's taking a journey from the Port of London, his ship won't be leaving until

the tide's full again."

"Then there's still time to catch him!" Ralph said. "That settles it. We won't have time to speak to Strange. We've got to get to the docks, and fast!"

# Chapter Nine

## To the Land of Liberty

Beth was immersed in water again, but this time it was steaming and welcome. She lay in the tavern's one and only tin bath in front of a heaped-up fire, relishing the warmth after her ordeal. She sighed in delight as Maisie poured another pail of hot water in. The lamplight flickered around them.

"Thanks, Maisie. This bath is bliss. I'm sorry to wake you up so late – or early!"

Maisie shook her head. "Gave me the fright of my life, you did. You looked half-drowned!"

Beth didn't need reminding. When Maisie had seen

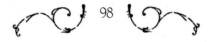

her standing in the doorway in the pre-dawn gloom, looking bedraggled as a sea-hag, she'd almost screamed the place down. Only Beth's swift reassurance had calmed her, along with a lie about how she'd slipped and fallen from the docks.

"What were you thinking, miss?" Maisie scolded, a frown creasing her brow in curiosity. "I wouldn't have gone down to those docks at this hour, not for all the tea in China."

"I know, I know. It's my fault I fell in. I wasn't paying attention." Beth was thankful Maisie didn't question her any further. The bathwater was almost as murky as the Thames now, but at least she felt human again. She rinsed off her hair while Maisie chatted away happily, none the worse now for having been woken up by her dripping friend in the middle of the night.

"You mustn't let me keep you up," Beth said. "You need to get some rest!"

"Oh, truth be told, I wasn't sleeping much anyway," beamed Maisie. "I'm too excited about my part."

"Your part?" Beth realized all at once that she'd not heard any theatre news for a while. She hadn't even asked Maisie about the results of the audition.

"I'm going to be Maid Marian in *Robin of the*

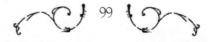

*Greenwood*!" Maisie said, grinning. "Can you imagine?"

"That's wonderful!" Beth exclaimed. "I knew you'd done well, but getting the female lead? I'm jealous!"

"Oh, please don't be jealous," Maisie said, her smile vanishing. "I'd never be as good as you, please don't think I—" The smile came back as she saw Beth was clearly joking. "Oh, Mistress Beth, you do tease."

Beth went to dry herself off and get dressed while Maisie walked back and forth, chattering. "They've cast Mister Lovett as the Sheriff, and of course he's happy with that – well, as happy as he ever is, I mean. And Samuel Jones was meant to be Robin, but he and Mister Lovett kept fighting so now Timothy Sewell's got the part instead, honestly, miss, you should have heard the language, it would have made you blush…" Beth let her carry on. It was amazing how theatre gossip built up, even over a scant few days.

"I'm so happy for you," Beth smiled, relieved to be in fresh clean clothes now.

"You really mean it?"

Beth took her hands. "Of course I do, silly! You sing beautifully, and the audience is going to *love* you, just wait and see. I bet you'll be the talk of London after opening night!"

"The talk of London," Maisie echoed. "Sometimes I do wonder, though, if this is really, truly right for me…" She pulled away from Beth and sat down, then turned to look out through the tiny window. London lights were twinkling in the dark.

"Maisie?" Beth sat beside her. "What's wrong?"

"I am happy, and the part is exciting, don't get me wrong. But … it's different for you, Mistress Beth," she said quietly. "London's your home."

"It's yours too."

"So why has it never *felt* like home?"

Beth was lost for words. Maisie was so quiet and serious all of a sudden. *How long had these feelings been stewing inside her?* she wondered. With a start, she realized how much she'd taken her young friend for granted.

"You're just getting a touch of nerves," Beth smiled, trying to sound reassuring. "Everyone gets those. It's your first big part. It's natural!"

Maisie heaved a sigh. "I know you're trying to be kind, but if I'm honest, I'm really not sure I want to stay here."

"But … you were so excited a moment ago!"

"And I am!" Maisie insisted. "I'm truly grateful, believe me! But it's made me think too. About what I really want to do. Where I really want to be."

101

Beth was shocked. Was she really hearing this? Maybe she still had water in her ears.

"I like London well enough, but it's just so crowded," Maisie went on. "You can't hear yourself think half the time. And the people can be so rude, looking down on you like you're nothing."

"Oh." Beth's heart sank. "So where would you like to be, if not here?"

Maisie gave a half-smile. "I keep thinking about America," she said. "I wish I had the words to tell you about it, Mistress Beth. I dream about it often." She closed her eyes. "Running through the cornfields when I was a little girl, out in the open air! Rope swing down by the creek, the jackrabbits scuttling away … Then I wake up, and it's all buildings and streets and people again."

"But don't you want to keep looking for your father?" was all Beth could say.

"That's just it," Maisie said in a tiny voice. "He's not here. All this time … it turns out he was never in London. He wasn't even in England."

Beth stared. "What? But I thought you'd been looking for him here all this time and—"

Maisie shook her head sadly. "Just the other day, I met a woman who'd just come back from transportation, after

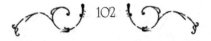

serving out her seven years in America," she explained. "She kept staring at me as if she'd seen a ghost. When I asked why, she said I was the very image of a man she'd seen in Virginia. 'Especially the eyes,' she told me. 'He had such blue eyes, just like you. They seemed to strike right to my soul.'"

"But that doesn't mean it was him, surely?"

A tear fell from Maisie's eye. "She said he was an Englishman, Mistress Beth. He'd gone to America to look … to look for…"

Beth's mouth fell open. She finished Maisie's sentence in a whisper. "To look for his little girl?"

Maisie nodded, her eyes brimming over with tears now. "All this time," she repeated, "I've been over here looking for *him*, while he's been over in America, looking for *me*! Maybe our ships even passed each other in the ocean!"

Beth gave her friend a tight hug. "You should have told me!"

"I only just found out," Maisie sniffled.

"Well then, if you must go, I understand completely," Beth said. "But I'd miss you, Maisie. I'd miss you terribly."

Maisie looked up at her suddenly, her eyes shining bright. "But I wouldn't want to leave you behind,

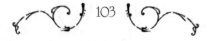

Mistress Beth! I was thinking perhaps we could go away *together*…"

Beth barely had time to register that new bombshell when there was a *tac* at the window. Someone had thrown a tiny stone at it, and Beth looked down into the street and saw Ralph looking up at her, readying another piece of grit. He waved frantically and pointed at a carriage, out of which John's head was poking.

"Oh … er … I have to go," she stammered. "It's some friends of mine from, er, a theatre out of town, come to visit. Their journey must have been quicker than they expected. I clean forgot all about it. I said I'd show them around London…"

She began to pull her boots on and Maisie silently helped her lace them up. If she had any doubts about Beth's story, she didn't voice them – she still seemed caught up in her thoughts about leaving. *Tac.* Another stone on the window.

"I'm coming as fast as I can," Beth muttered through clenched teeth.

"You'll think about what I said?" Maisie looked serious.

"I promise I will," Beth said, wishing she didn't have to. The idea of leaving London was just too big to think about right now…

* * *

Moments later, Beth flung herself into the back of the carriage. The leather seats were icy cold. John and Ralph's faces were almost hidden by shadow.

"Where are we going? Did you find something out?" she said. "Are we going to see Strange?"

"There's no time," John said excitedly. "'The game is afoot!'"

"This ain't no game," Ralph snapped.

"It's Shakespeare," Beth said, rolling her eyes. "John means it's time to chase the prey to ground."

"Should have ruddy said so, then," Ralph muttered, folding his arms.

"We worked out the truth about *Dorcas*," John explained to Beth, ignoring him. "She's a *ship*, one that Vale's booked onto. I checked the records in the Naval office and found out where she's berthed, and we were close by so we thought we'd come and get you before high tide hits."

"We're going to try and catch Vale? Without telling Strange first?"

John nodded. "It's our one chance. We have to bring him down."

105

Beth understood – she only hoped Strange would understand too. Doing this was a gamble, but she agreed it was a chance they had to take.

The driver drove the horses so hard that pedestrians were shouting and shaking their fists as the carriage raced through London. They nearly toppled over when they charged around corners. Once, years ago, Beth had seen the mangled aftermath of a coach overturning, and she tried to shut the image of the wreckage out of her mind. John didn't seem to care about the danger, though. He kept his head stuck out of the carriage window, and soon he was yelling, "We're at the docks! We can still make it!"

The three of them piled out of the carriage and out onto the open dockside. Dawn was just beginning to steal up over the sky, and masts swayed and rigging creaked. In the breaking light, they could see at least five ships that might be the one they were looking for.

"Excuse me," Beth said breathlessly to a red-eyed dockworker struggling with a crate. "Which of these is the *Dorcas*?"

"None of them," the man grunted. "If you wanted to board her, you're too late. She's just set sail." He pointed down the length of the Thames to where a large ship was sailing away, almost out of sight in the morning mists.

Beth's heart sank, and she heard Ralph curse under his breath.

She thought quickly. "Do you know where she's bound for?"

The dockworker laughed. "You'll have a long swim if you want to catch her, young lady. The *Dorcas* is bound for America."

The three of them stood on the quay and watched the ship vanish from sight, fading into the distance like an impossible dream. Their prey was gone. Nobody spoke. What would have been the point? There was nothing more to say.

Vale was gone.

# Chapter Ten

## Desperate Measures

It was the morning of the next day and John was nearly home. In one hand, thrust deep into his pocket, he clutched the single coin that was all that remained of his wages. The landlord had scowled at him when he'd knocked, but his expression had quickly changed when John had handed over the money he'd earned from watching Vale's tower. It had taken care of the arrears, and now at least the heavies would be called off. Whatever else might happen, his family wouldn't be out on the street.

Vale might have been on his way to America and

Strange furious that they'd let their quarry slip away, but John still smiled to himself as he thought that he'd spared his mother the nightmare of an eviction, for now. He had seen evictions before. They were horrible – the furniture piled up in the street, the children sobbing, the grim-faced men carting treasured possessions off to be sold, the neighbours peering out of their windows to sneak a look. No wonder some people stole and cheated just to scrape money together for the rent.

He pushed the front door open and strode into the single room that served as both kitchen and dining room. "Morning, everyone! I've been to Mister Clatherton and paid the rent…"

His voice died away as he saw his family gathered round the table, looking up at him with darkened eyes and pinched-looking faces. Nobody had the energy to celebrate his good news. His mother came over to him urgently. "John?" she croaked. "You've brought money?"

"I … I paid the rent," he repeated helplessly. How could they have fallen so far? He'd only been away for a few days. At the back of the room, his father lay in his bed. They must have brought it downstairs. The bandages on his hand were filthy now, matted through with stains that made John feel sick just to look at.

The infection must have worsened.

John held out the single penny that he had. His mother snatched it out of his hand and rushed out, calling, "I-I'll bring food."

"There's been nothing to eat," Nick explained. "Not for days."

"But hasn't anyone helped?" John said incredulously. "The neighbours … the vicar?"

Nick shook his head. "Everyone's got troubles of their own, is what they're saying."

John sat at the table and buried his face in his hands. This was all wrong. He should have taken all the money home right away, instead of going to pay the rent. The landlord could have waited another week for his money, couldn't he? What was the use of a place to live if you didn't even have food?

The door banged open and his mother came rushing back in carrying a tiny loaf of bread. A penny loaf, they called them, not much bigger than a bun, but she was clutching it like a new-born baby. Chairs scraped and the children stood up, and his mother carefully broke off pieces to give to each of them, and to his father. In seconds the loaf was gone, and his mother stood desperately licking the crumbs from her fingers. She saw

John's look of dismay and instantly dissolved into tears.

"What are we going to do?" she sobbed.

John gently put his arm round her, and he could feel her shoulder blades protruding under her thin skin.

"I'll work all the hours God sends," he said. "Whatever it takes, Mother."

"Bless you," she said. "I know you're trying your best, love. But there just aren't enough hours in the day."

It was true. John couldn't hope to make up for his father's lost wages, even if he took every spying mission Strange offered. As he watched Polly hobbling across the room on her crutches to give his father his medicine, a terrible thought came to him. With Vale gone, would there even *be* any more spying missions? That decided him. He had to take drastic action.

"I'll be back soon," he promised, and headed out of the house.

He set off, walking resolutely towards the open vegetable market. His family needed food, fast. And he was going to get it. He just needed to figure out how. What did other people do when their families were desperately hungry? Some of them stole, of course. London was riddled with thieves, but he wasn't going to take that path. "I'd sooner hang," he muttered. Begging?

That wasn't much better than stealing, in John's book. Plenty of people begged because they had no other choice: the diseased, the blind, the wounded veterans of England's many wars … No. Begging wasn't an option either. For one thing, John thought bitterly, he was able-bodied. People would just tell him to get a job, and walk on by.

The only thing for it was to scavenge what he could. He'd often noticed fruit and vegetables rolling away while the traders set up their stands. The traders never bothered to chase after them, it wasn't worth their while. Maybe, if nobody else had already snatched them up, he could find a fallen potato or even a cabbage. The thought of his family eating food from the dirty floor made him grimace, but he couldn't see what other choice they had.

The market stalls were bustling, and the traders could hardly keep up with the number of people shouting and waving money. John moved up alongside an apple-seller. The fruit lay crimson and gold on the trays, looking tempting and delicious. It would be so easy to grab one, just one, but John shook his head. *Never.*

He squeezed past the row of stalls into the blind alley beyond, where refuse had been piled up. Nobody

seemed to mind him being there – they all had paying customers to think about. Trying not to make it too obvious, he wandered up and down, glancing at the pavement. Straight away, he saw a flash of yellow at his feet – a dropped apple! He picked it up, delighted with his find. There was a brown bruise on one side and it was smeared with roadside mud, but that didn't matter. He could rinse it off. He slipped it into his pocket, whistling a merry jig. Sometimes, he thought to himself, you have to make your own luck. A few more minutes of hunting netted him half a potato and some cabbage leaves that would be wholesome enough once the bad bits were cut off.

But down beside the cabbage, he noticed something grey and smooth. He frowned. Perhaps it was a mushroom? But when he picked it up, he saw it was a length of dangling silk. A handkerchief attached to a button, and a very fine quality one. Perhaps one of the traders had dropped it. He looked around, but instantly dismissed that idea. The traders were all working people, with no use for anything so fancy. He had a better look at it. It was clean, so it must have been dropped very recently. Thinking of Vale's monogrammed kerchiefs, he turned it around in his hands, looking for similar initials,

but there weren't any.

"This could be the windfall to end all windfalls," he whispered to himself. There was a tailor not far from here who'd pay good money for this. And he hadn't stolen it – he'd just found it lying there. So why not sell it? Anyone else would, without a second thought, and the money could keep his family fed for a week. *But it isn't mine to sell*, he thought.

Surely the owner must still be nearby. He took another look at the crowds surrounding the fruit stalls, but they all seemed to be local people who were buying for themselves, or maids out buying for the families they served. A handkerchief like this must belong to a gentleman, and gentlemen didn't buy their own groceries. So … perhaps someone had pickpocketed it elsewhere and then dropped it? John decided to take it to the local Watch, who could look out for its owner, and tucked it into his pocket along with the apple, potato and cabbage leaves. He smiled as he thought of the owner going to talk to the Watch, of his flustered expression changing to joy, of the reward he might receive…

"Hey!" came a shout from behind him. "You there!"

"Hmm?" John turned round. An officious-looking man came running up to him and grabbed him

by the shoulder.

"Ow!" John said, struggling. "What do you think you're—"

"I," panted the red-faced man, "am the beadle of this market! And I have reason to believe," he paused for breath, "that there is something in your pocket that doesn't belong to you!"

# Chapter Eleven

## Taken

In her dreams, Beth was in the wooden chest again. This time, John and Ralph couldn't get it open, and water was flooding into her lungs. She struggled, growing weaker and weaker, as Ralph banged desperately at the lock. She groaned and rolled over opening her eyes.

Suddenly she was wide-awake. The bedclothes were tangled around her, but the frantic banging was still going on. Beth sat up. Someone was hammering at the door of their lodgings. Across the room, Maisie was sitting up too, rubbing her eyes.

"Who is it?"

Beth didn't say what she was thinking. There was only one person who had reason to visit her like this, with no regard for the time of night. Only one person who could be angry enough with her to hammer on her door as if he meant to break it down. She'd known this was coming ever since they'd let Vale get away, but she was not going to expose Maisie to Strange's anger. The girl wasn't a part of her life as a spy and Beth wasn't about to let that change.

"Stay there," she warned Maisie. She lit a candle with a taper from the embers of the fire and went to open the door.

But it wasn't Strange.

It was some lunatic off the streets, with tousled hair and urgent, staring eyes. He rushed into the room, grabbing Beth by the shoulders. Beth yelled in surprise and nearly dropped the candle. Then, as she held it steady, she recognized the youth for the first time.

"Ralph!"

"I need to talk to you," he said, in a voice like cold iron. "On your own, right now."

"It's all right!" Beth said to Maisie, who was peering fearfully down the stairs, and Big Moll, the inn's owner, who was looking more angry at being woken.

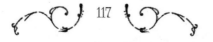

117

"I know him. Go back to bed. Everything's fine." They turned away, with Moll muttering to herself. Beth turned back to Ralph. "Sit down by the fire. You must be freezing."

"There's no time," Ralph said. He strode back and forth angrily. "My contacts had bad news for me tonight. It's John. He's been taken."

Beth's heart skipped a beat. "Taken? By whom? Vale's men?"

"No. The Watch! He's been arrested on suspicion of stealing," Ralph said, spitting out the words as if they were poisoned. "They're holding him in a cell."

"Where?" asked Beth firmly.

"Bridewell." Ralph looked at Beth to see if she knew what that word meant. Her look of horror surely told him she knew only too well. *Bridewell.* That word sent chills through Beth. As prisons went, it was downright medieval. What with the filth, the rats and the disease, not to mention the brutality of the inmates toward one another, it was almost a death sentence in itself.

"We need to go and see him right away," she said. "There must be something we can do. Have you told Strange?"

"No. Not yet. I came straight to you."

Beth ran upstairs and hurriedly pulled her street clothes on. The charge had to be false, she thought hopefully. It's all a misunderstanding and they'd let him off. John wouldn't steal.

She said a quick goodbye to Maisie, saying everything would be fine, and together she and Ralph rushed out into the night. It wasn't far to Bridewell Prison. As it loomed into view, Beth wondered how such a gloomy, hateful building could ever have been a royal palace. That had been long ago, back in the days of Henry VIII. Now it was an asylum for the insane, a workhouse and a prison, all in one.

To Beth's dismay, the keeper demanded a fee to let her in. "Everything costs," he said with a sneer. "If he's that important to you, you'll find the money."

Beth silently handed over the shilling. "Take us to see him *now*," she said, barely containing her anger.

"No hurry," the keeper chuckled. "He's not going anywhere. He's still got his chains on." He held up a hand to Ralph's chest. "Just the girl." Ralph scowled, but let Beth go on ahead.

John was one of seven tattered, grimy figures in the cell they eventually reached. Some of his cellmates smirked

to see him rush forward. "Who is it, Turner?" one of them mocked. "Your mother come to see you again so soon?" But their smiles turned to scowls of jealousy when Beth pulled her hood back and showed her face.

"John! Why are you still manacled?" Beth said in a low voice. "It's inhumane. I'll fetch a guard and have you released."

"You have to pay to have your chains removed," John said. "You have to pay for everything in here."

"Being a keeper's good money, miss," sneered one of the prisoners.

Beth simply ignored him. "Tell me what happened, John."

John explained how he had found the handkerchief while hunting for food. His cellmates looked on, obviously amused by the tale.

"I told them I hadn't stolen it," he said. "I said I was taking it to the Watch so the owner could come and get it. But the more I said, the less they believed me. They called me a pickpocket!"

"And the owner never came forward?"

"No," John said. "It was like they *wanted* me to be a thief. 'Caught one of you at last,' they said. 'We'll make an example of you.'"

That made sense, Beth thought. She'd read angry headlines in the *London Gazette* about thievery in the city, especially in the markets. The cry had been going up for weeks now for the government to get tough on crime, and Beth had the uneasy feeling that even an innocent victim would still send a message.

"They won't find you guilty," she said. "This is a civilized country. We have courts, not mob rule!"

A chorus of laughter came from the prisoners then, all except John. Beth glared at them.

"I hope you're right," John said, leaning close so he could speak softly. "Because stealing is a capital offence. If they do find me guilty, they'll likely hang me…"

*It will be all right*, she wanted to tell him. *I'll get Strange to help.* But, of course, she couldn't say anything like that, not here.

Within moments it was time to leave, and as she reached the top of the stairs, Beth looked back and saw John's gaunt face. His jaw was set, but his eyes were those of a man whose world is crumbling into ruin around him.

"I will do everything in my power to help you," she promised. *Right now, no price is too high to save my friend*, she thought.

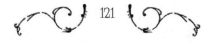

* * *

"You wanted to see me, sir?"

Beth waited by the chair opposite Strange in Peake's Coffee House. As yet, despite the new trend for coffee-drinking, London society had yet to declare this place "fashionable", so it was discreet enough to serve as a meeting place. All the tables were taken up by middle-aged men in large wigs, discussing serious matters with bowed heads or playing games of chess. The thick aroma of ground coffee filled the air, and nobody spoke louder than a soft murmur. It was like the reading room of a library, or some strange chapel where tobacco smoke hung in clouds instead of incense.

Beth stood, trembling, waiting for Strange to meet her eye, but he just gestured for her to sit.

"You understand I do not hold you responsible for his escape, but we need to reconsider our plans, now that Vale has fled."

"Yes, sir. We really did do everything in our power to stop him."

"I know." Strange sipped from a gigantic bowl of black coffee. "And I still believe that you, Ralph Chandler and

122

John Turner make a good team, one that I would like to employ again—"

"Then you haven't heard? John's in prison!" Beth burst out. "They're holding him for the theft of a silk handkerchief, but he didn't steal it, he just found it!" she began, feeling that she was babbling but unable to stop herself.

"Prison," said Strange, pressing his knuckles to his forehead. "I had, of course, heard report of this, but I hoped it mere rumour. That's exceedingly inconvenient, but it could play to our advantage..."

Taken aback by his tone, Beth said, "So ... is there anything you can do?"

Strange looked at her. "It may be better for now to do nothing at all."

"What? Sir, forgive me, but ... but we need to save him! Surely you won't let a valuable spy be kept in prison, or ... or worse!" Beth exclaimed. "Don't you understand? He ... he might be executed!"

"Lower your voice, Miss Johnson," Strange said in a warning tone. "Listen. Time is limited and there are plans in motion that you know nothing about. Trust me. I will help, even if I seem to be doing nothing."

There was a moment of cold silence between them

123

then. *My mistake*, Beth thought. *For a second there I confused you with a human being. It won't happen again.*

"I had something specific to discuss with you," Strange eventually said. "In the light of Vale's flight from the country, I have given serious thought to your future as an operative under my supervision."

Beth braced herself for what was coming next. Strange took another long sip of coffee before continuing.

"It's extremely unlikely that Vale leaving the country means his anti-royal days are over," Strange said. "He has organized plots from abroad before, for example when he was in Germany, as you know."

Beth nodded, remembering Vale's pawn Lady Lucy Joseph. Or Luzi Bayer, which had been her real name...

"Vale is far too dangerous to leave unobserved. He plays a long game, setting up power bases long before he moves to a new centre of operations. We need to move with him if we are to thwart him."

This wasn't what Beth had expected to hear at all. "Move with him? Do you have a spy network in America?"

"No," Strange said, mopping at his mouth with a pure white napkin. "And that's the point. We need one. I need people in America I can count on to watch Vale

and report back to me regularly. There are people there now, of course, but they aren't the *right* people."

Beth suddenly wasn't sure if she felt like a hunted animal in the sights of a crossbow, or a young hopeful about to be called up to a starring role. "Do you mean…?"

"I've been looking for the right person to head up a spy network for some time," Strange said. His eyes were eager and bright now. He began to count off on his fingers. "Someone young, who isn't set in their ways, someone who can learn, but has proven themselves as uniquely adept in this field. They'd be based in America for months, possibly even years, so they can't have important family or career ties here in England. Does this sound like anyone you know?"

Only her training as an actor allowed Beth to answer him calmly. Inside, she was shaking like a fever victim. "You have me in mind? I have to admit I'm surprised you'd trust such an enterprise to a young *woman*." She raised an eyebrow, a smile playing at the edge of her lips.

Strange sat back in his chair and interlaced his fingers. "As I say, you're uniquely suited. And nobody would suspect you of being a spy. I'll put it to you straight. How would you feel about going to America as the first ever head of my operations in the New World?"

"Uh … I'll need more information first," Beth said after a pause. That got a smile of approval from Strange. Beth didn't say what she'd been thinking: *I thought you'd summoned me here to* fire *me, not promote me!*

"You would still be acting under my instruction, of course," he said. "You'd be travelling undercover, playing the role of a lady of means. However, all other arrangements – recruiting spies, establishing safe houses and so on – would be entirely at your discretion. You would have a great deal of freedom, and the salary is extremely generous."

Beth reeled under the impact of all this. "How long do I have to think about it?"

"I want your answer within the week," the spymaster told her. "We haven't lost Vale. You could be hot on his trail in a matter of days, following him across the Atlantic. But you'll have to move fast."

"I see."

Strange stood up. As far as he was concerned, the meeting was finished. "Think it over," he said. "When you've made your decision, contact me. You know the protocol. Good day."

Then he was gone, and Beth was left alone with her thoughts.

# Chapter Twelve

## As One Door Closes...

Beth could see that Maisie had been waiting for her back at the Peacock and Pie. The young girl leaped to her feet as soon as she heard Beth come in. "Is there any news on your friend?"

*Oh, there's news all right, and I only wish I could tell you*, thought Beth.

"They're hearing his case this afternoon at Bow Street Court," Beth said. "They'll find him innocent. They have to."

"I'll go along with you," Maisie volunteered.

Beth wasn't sure if it was a good idea. There was

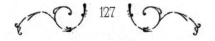

always the risk of her work as a spy being exposed when her fellow agents were in the picture, and she tried to protect Maisie from being involved. "But surely you have to rehearse?" she hedged.

"Honestly, Mistress Beth. You're always running around looking after people, never a thought for yourself. This time, you're the one who needs some support."

Her friend's loyalty nearly brought tears to Beth's eyes. Looking at her serious face, she knew she couldn't keep quiet a moment longer. "Maisie … thank you, but I'll be fine. In fact, there's other news. Big, big news."

Maisie's eyes widened. "Yes?"

"I've been offered a new position. There'd be plenty of money, along with lots of responsibility." She took a breath. "And it'd be in America."

"Oh my goodness!" Maisie burst out. "What are the chances? What is it? Acting? Teaching? You're going to be a governess?" Then she stopped and a look of fresh amazement covered her face. "Mistress Beth. I know what this is. You're getting married to a rich merchant, aren't you?"

"No!" Beth said in horror, then burst out laughing, with Maisie joining in. "Can you imagine me married to some terrible old moneybags?" Beth spluttered.

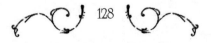

"Well, it's none of my business what your position would be, I'm sure," Maisie said, a hint of sadness in her voice now. "I just wish I had some way to come with you."

"And *I* wish I could tell you all about it," Beth said. "But the details are still being worked out. Once everything is signed and sealed, I'll tell you more, I promise."

"Well, whatever it is, I'm just so happy for you!" Maisie said. "It's beautiful out there. You can't do it justice unless you've seen it with your own eyes. You can really make something of yourself out there." Her voice grew smaller. "I only hope that's what my father's doing…"

"Oh, Maisie," Beth said, squeezing her friend's hand. "Anyway, perhaps I might stay. I already have made something of myself, right here in London." She sighed. "You make it sound so inviting. But my acting has gone from strength to strength here. What about my admirers, all the people who come to see me every week? How can I let them down? I'd be throwing away so much!"

"Oh, Mistress Beth, how can I put this?" Maisie frowned. "I think you might be more loyal to them than they are to you."

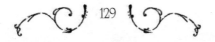 129

"What do you mean?"

"Now, don't take this the wrong way, but women on the London stage don't last nearly as long as men. It's all very well when you're sixteen and the companies are willing to take a chance on you, but by the time you're past twenty, everyone's whispering that you ought to get married and settle down. It ain't exactly a respectable career for an older woman, if you take my meaning."

"I'll get married in my own time," Beth said fiercely, "if I ever do."

"But it ain't all about what you want, miss," Maisie said gently. "You're not in charge. Mister Huntingdon is."

"I don't need reminding," Beth muttered.

"Although…" Maisie's voice trailed off.

"Yes?"

"Nothing. It's foolish of me."

"Maisie," Beth said, "What's on your mind?"

"If you did go to America, you could always be an actress there as well," Maisie said. "And with a whole new country to set up in – why, you could do what you've always wanted and found your *own* company!"

"My own company," Beth echoed. She *could* do it. Even when she grew too old for the stage, she had always

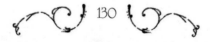

imagined she could manage other actors. No more compromises, no more taking direction … *no more Lovett*! That, alongside Strange's offer? Head of both her own spy network *and* her own theatre company? It could be perfect. Suddenly Beth saw herself living two brilliant lives, completely in control of both: directing shadowy agents and assigning them missions, directing young actors and assigning them their parts. She would be a spymistress like the world had never seen.

"You're right, Maisie. Why *shouldn't* I do it?" she said, jumping from her chair and walking around the room as her excitement grew. "The world's bigger than London, after all! All the companies here are always trying to outdo us. They steal our scripts, they poach our stars and our audiences … but in America, we could start from scratch!"

"If it was me, I'd do it in a heartbeat," Maisie said.

"I've no family here," Beth said. For once in her life, that struck her as a good thing. She'd been a foundling baby. "None but you, of course, Maisie. You're like a sister to me."

Maisie hugged her. "I love you too. But you mustn't let that hold you back, Mistress Beth—"

"I wonder…" Beth said quietly, and then looked

Maisie in the eye suddenly. "What if there *were* a way to bring you with me?"

Maisie's mouth was a perfect O of amazement. *If I'm to be travelling as a grand lady*, Beth thought, *I'll need a maid. Who better than Maisie to play the part? Surely Strange could be persuaded to see the sense in that?*

"I can't promise, but I think I may know a way," Beth said. "Let me speak to the people in charge. I'll do what I can—"

"Oh! Oh, Mistress Beth!" Maisie cried, not seeming to register the caution in Beth's words. She span on the spot and burst out singing: "I'll be sailin' away from old England's fair shore, to the land where tobacco grows high…"

But as Maisie went on to the verse about the laddie she left behind back in old London town, Beth realized her mind wasn't completely made up after all. There was one thing about Strange's offer she had overlooked. Even if John's neck somehow escaped the hangman's noose, he'd still be here in England while Beth was far across the cold Atlantic in America. If she accepted Strange's offer, she might never see him again.

Unless, of course, Strange knew more than he had told…

# Chapter Thirteen

**Crime and Punishment**

The cell where John sat was barely larger than a cupboard and stank like a latrine. Straw had been scattered on the floor, as if this was a place to keep beasts rather than people. A filthy bucket stood to one side. John didn't look at it.

His cell was only one in a row of eight. They were beneath the Old Bailey, him and the seven other prisoners, waiting to be called up to their trials. Guards had frog-marched him out of Bridewell at dawn, chained to the others, and they had been carted up here in a jolting wagon and thrown into their cells. Then there

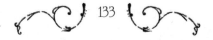

was nothing to do but wait.

A few of the other prisoners talked to him. The first question was always the same: "What are you up for?" In this way, he learned his fellow prisoners had been arrested for drunkenness, arson, public brawling, disturbance of the peace and similar crimes. They didn't seem surprised to hear he'd been arrested for stealing. John didn't bother to protest his innocence. He'd quickly learned at Bridewell that *everyone* in prison insisted they were innocent. Not long after they arrived, the guards began to drag them upstairs one by one. The first to be taken was the public drunkard, Jimmy. John had rather liked the white-whiskered man, who had tried to make a joke of it, holding out his hands for the guards to cuff while saying, "Take me away, boys. Rather face you than me wife." But when he was brought back down ten minutes later he had tears in his eyes.

"Guilty," said the man in the cell to John's left; Leonard, the supposed arsonist. "That's a fine he can't afford. He'll be in the poorhouse after this, poor old devil."

Next, the guards took Morton, a sailor whose only language seemed to be swear words. He was brought back even more swiftly than Jimmy, shouting and struggling all the way.

"He started it!" he bellowed. "I was defendin' myself! You've no right!"

"Shut up," the guard said wearily. "Any more noise out of you and you'll lose your tongue."

"That's another guilty one," Leonard said wearily.

One by one, the other prisoners were taken up then brought back down, with the same story every time. And each time John heard the guards come back down the stairs, his stomach lurched. He went over what he would say to the judge in his mind, repeating it to himself. Eventually only he and Leonard were left.

The other man went quietly, giving John a wink.

"Cheer up," he said. "Got to put on a brave face, don't yer?"

"Good luck!" John said softly. But when the guards brought Leonard back down again soon afterward, the man was shaking. He said nothing as the guards closed the cell door. John wondered if he should say anything as Leonard sat there, staring at his shoes. The pressure of silence grew and grew until John couldn't bear it.

"So … what did you get?" he asked.

"Guilty," said Leonard. "I'm to be hanged by the neck. Until I'm dead."

John tried to say something, but the words didn't make it past his throat. It was as if a rope was choking him. "I'm sorry," he stammered eventually. Leonard turned away and stared at the wall.

When John heard the guards coming, he was on his feet in a second. Being in the presence of a condemned man was giving him the horrors.

"Turner," the guard said. "You're next."

John didn't struggle, doing his best to keep up with their pace, but it wasn't easy with his legs chained together. He stumbled once, and got a whack in the ribs for it. Finally they emerged into the courtroom, and John's innards were in a tight knot as he saw the stern faces of the jurors lined up on both sides of the room, the prosecutor in his box and the judge looking down with a bored expression. The guards dragged him to the dock and shoved him inside. John blinked. Light was shining right into his eyes. A big mirror had been set up above the court to shine light from the windows down onto his face. He realized it must be so the jury could get a good look at the witness's expression. It made him feel as if Heaven itself was accusing him.

*I've done nothing wrong*, he reminded himself.

Unfriendly eyes were glaring at him from all sides.

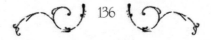

But no – someone was waving from the public gallery, off to the side. It was Beth. He managed a smile and she rewarded him with a huge, supportive smile of her own. He knew his mother wouldn't have been able to handle seeing him before the judge, but he was glad to have Beth there.

The judge wasn't impressed at his smiling, and gave John a raven-black stare, then rapped his gavel to call the court to order.

"Court is now in session," he droned. "John Turner, you will take the oath."

His hand on the Bible, John swore to tell the truth, the whole truth and nothing but the truth.

"You stand accused of the crime of pickpocketing, the goods in question being a silk handkerchief, value eighteen pence. How do you plead?"

"Not guilty," John said clearly.

The judge rolled his eyes. "Very well. Mister Shadwell will now lead the prosecution."

Shadwell was a brisk young man who couldn't have been much older than John. "I wish to call Mister Blavistock, beadle of Cheapside Market, to the witness stand."

The beadle came huffing up, took his place at the

stand and pointed at John. "It was 'im, Your Honour. I saw him. He done it."

"I have not yet asked you any questions, Mister Blavistock," Shadwell reminded him, crooking a smile. Some of the jurors tittered at that.

"Beg your pardon," the beadle said.

John was powerless to do anything. He knew he couldn't interrupt or make a scene. That would only work against him. So he sat tight-lipped as Shadwell prompted Blavistock to tell his damning tale.

"Tell the court what you saw."

"Well, the accused was hanging about behind the market stalls, acting all suspicious-like. Looking about, sir. Like he was waiting for an opportunity."

That set the jury to muttering. The judge gave his gavel a warning rap to hush them.

"When you saw the accused holding the handkerchief, how would you say he looked?"

"Happy, sir," said Blavistock. "Like he'd got away with it."

"I see," said Shadwell. "Now, I understand that you did not observe the actual theft?"

"With respect, sir, there were lots of people coming and going."

 138

"But as an experienced beadle of ten years' standing, you are confident that a theft took place?"

Blavistock shrugged. "One minute he didn't have it, the next he did. It don't take a genius to work it out, sir, to my way of thinking. I mean, he didn't take it out of his *own* pocket, did he?"

"Master Turner doesn't seem like the type to afford silk kerchiefs, I agree!" smirked Shadwell. Laughs came from the public gallery, and the jury nodded vigorously, to John's dismay.

"Tell me, Mister Blavistock; is pickpocketing a common crime around the market?"

Blavistock nodded, looking disgusted. "These kids, they have it down to a fine art. People like me, we work as hard as we can to stop 'em, but there's just too many! Like rats!"

Shadwell smirked at this. After some more banter between him and Blavistock, it was finally time for John to give his own account.

"Do you deny that you were loitering behind the stalls?" Shadwell opened.

"I was looking for food," John said. His cheeks burned with the shame of it. "Not to steal. I'm not a thief."

"The jury will note that the accused denies being

a thief," Shadwell said, with a note of mock surprise. "If you were not planning to steal, where was this food meant to come from?"

"From the gutter," John said, unable to contain his anger. "I thought I might find some goods that had fallen off the stalls, stuff nobody else wanted. I picked up a bruised apple and some cabbage leaves."

"And the silk handkerchief? I suppose that came from the gutter too?"

"Yes," John said stubbornly. Shadwell was making the truth sound like a lie.

The prosecutor strode over and leaned his elbow on the edge of the dock.

"Hunger and poverty lead men to do desperate things, don't they, Turner?"

"I suppose," John said. He had the uncomfortable feeling he was being led into a trap.

"You suppose? Let's look at your own situation. Your father lost his job recently following a terrible injury. Your family – a *large* family, at that – is in desperate need of food—"

"That doesn't make me a thief!" John protested.

Beth watched all this with a sinking heart. Beside her, a woman was knitting – she seemed to be here for the

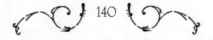

entertainment, and turned to her companion. "Guilty as hell, that one," she murmured. "It's obvious. God knows we've all had hungry children at home before, and *we've* never resorted to stealing.

Her companion nodded. "I blame the parents."

"How dare you?" Beth hissed.

"Eh?" the woman said.

"John Turner is my friend!" Beth snarled. "He'd never, ever do anything dishonest! You say one more word against him, and I'll take those knitting needles and ram them so hard—"

The woman stared at Beth, shocked and clutching her knitting as if to hide behind it.

"Order in court!" the judge called, hammering with his gavel, noticing their escalating confrontation. Smouldering, Beth sat back down. The two older women got up and went to sit on the other side of the public gallery.

"No further questions, Your Honour," said Shadwell, looking smug.

The jury took less than five minutes to come to their verdict.

John sat waiting for the announcement, feeling tense and sick to his stomach. He felt like he was already on

the gallows with a rope around his neck, just waiting for the trapdoor to drop away from beneath him.

"There's still a chance," he whispered to himself. "Hold fast."

"And what verdict have you reached?" the judge was asking the foreman.

"We find the defendant … *guilty*."

John felt the floor give way beneath him.

"John Turner," said the judge, "you have been found guilty of pickpocketing. I shall now pronounce sentence."

*Please*, John prayed silently. *My family needs me … please.*

"I shall not, on this occasion, impose the death penalty," the judge said. "Given that the goods in question are valued at a mere eighteen pence."

The knitting woman tutted loudly.

"Instead," the judge went on, "I sentence you to transportation. You will be shipped to America to serve a term of seven years, during which time you will not return to England on pain of death." The gavel banged. "Take him away."

# Chapter Fourteen

**Laying Plans**

Beth returned to the Peacock and Pie, feeling as if she had been turned to stone. "How could they think he was guilty?" she murmured, almost to herself.

"You have to look on the bright side," Maisie said, coming over and taking Beth's hand, squeezing it tight. "They could have hanged your friend, you know!"

Beth clenched her fist in frustrated rage. "It's not fair," she whispered. "Transportation? After everything he's done for this country…"

"What do you mean?" Maisie enquired, and Beth quickly shook her head, realizing her slip-up.

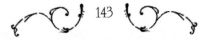

"Nothing … Uh, his work at the Navy Board." She sighed. "It's all just so unfair." Beth could hardly believe that Strange had done nothing, and now John had been found guilty of a crime he hadn't committed, would *never* have committed. Surely he could have done something, pulled some strings? She clenched her jaw angrily.

"Now, you pull yourself together, Mistress Beth," Maisie said sternly. "There's a lot worse than transportation, and I should know." Her voice softened. "It's not so bad. If you work hard, you can afford a few privileges. That sweetens life a bit. And it's only seven years. He can come back home once it's up. Or he can stay and make a new life for himself over there, like we hope to!"

"A new life," Beth repeated, thinking.

"He's young and strong. Well-spoken too. Your friend could really prosper in America." Maisie smiled encouragingly. "Think how much money he could send home to his family! Why, they might even buy their own house, in time. They couldn't do that on the pittance he likely earns here in London, could they? Don't worry, Mistress Beth. I'm sure someone's looking out for him. A guardian angel."

Beth sat up straight. Suddenly everything she had

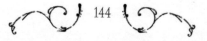

just seen made perfect sense. "That crafty old fox knew exactly what he was doing…!" she murmured to herself. John *did* have someone watching out for him; but "angel" certainly wasn't the word for Sir Alan Strange…

"I need to talk to you."

Strange rose from his armchair at the Corinthian Club. "Close the door."

Beth did so, leaving the two of them alone together in the darkened room. A single oil lamp stood on Strange's table, turned down low; the man liked the shadows.

"John Turner has been sentenced to transportation. But you already knew that would happen, didn't you?"

"I have saved his life," Strange said. "Soon he will be in America, ready to resume his career as an undercover spy. As will your colleague Ralph."

"Ralph too?" Beth exclaimed.

"He has agreed to form part of my new American spy network. I already have passage arranged for him. He would prefer to take up his spy work under your supervision, but as you haven't yet accepted my offer, I could not guarantee him that."

*Well played*, Beth thought.

"I've ... I've decided to accept, that offer, sir." Strange smiled, and Beth held up a hand. "But I have two conditions."

"Conditions?" Strange said, sounding both surprised and irritated.

"Yes. Firstly I require you to pay John Turner his first year's wages in advance."

Strange's irritation turned to anger as he saw she was serious. "My budget is limited, as you know very well. Why would I agree to such a thing?"

"Because I doubt any of your other senior agents is willing to uproot their whole life and move to America. More importantly, because John has a family who will starve without him," Beth said severely. "They cannot wait until he reaches America. They need the money *now*."

"I see," said Strange.

"My second condition is that I am allowed to bring a friend with me."

Strange sighed. "Let me guess. The orange girl," he said, not hiding his displeasure.

"Her name is Maisie. If I am travelling in disguise as a grand lady, then I will need a maid. She's perfect."

"And how on earth would you explain to her why you want her to play such a part?"

"Leave that to me."

Strange loomed above her, his face etched with shadows. "Miss Johnson, had you considered changing career? Perhaps your interest in worthy causes would be better served if you were patroness of a charitable institution."

Beth drew a deep breath. "We have nothing further to discuss," she said. "Good day, sir." She turned on her heel.

Her hand was on the doorknob when Strange called back to her. "Wait!"

"I was a foundling child," Beth said, without looking round at him. "Do *not* joke with me about charity, sir. I would not be here now without them."

"Miss Johnson…"

"Good day!"

"I'll grant your blasted conditions," Strange said quickly. "If that's the price I have to pay to get my network started in America, then so be it."

Beth nodded, stifling a smile. "Then we have a deal."

"We do. Meet me here tomorrow and we will finalize our plans. But I warn you, Miss Johnson, I am still your

superior. In future I will not be bargained with like a market fishwife!"

"Understood, sir."

Beth left without looking back, wearing a smile of victory on her face.

The man on the bench was dying, and he was doing it noisily.

"When's the beast?" he raved, whipping his head from side to side. "My lungs do bleat like buttered peas. O, laddie, whet me a moonbeam for to cut my way out…"

He had been raving like this for hours. The final stages of gaol fever had taken hold of him. Sores had spread across his face and he reeked like a slaughterhouse. John kept his distance as best he could. Here in the condemned block at Bridewell, the prisoners were crammed in like the human cargo on a slave ship. A semicircle had formed around the dying man as guards and prisoners alike watched him die.

"Where's my Dolly-o?" the man said, sitting bolt upright. Then his eyes rolled back in his head and he fell back. He made some wet sounds in his throat and his

breathing came to a slow, rattling end.

"There's another one we don't have to hang," one of the guards said. "Back away now, you filth. Show's over."

As they dragged the corpse away to a freshly dug lime pit, John heard the clang of a stick on a bucket. That meant food. Along with the other prisoners, he went to stand in line by the crude tables where the rations were being handed out. The man in front of John was given a large hunk of bread and a chicken leg to chew, along with a mug of beer. The other prisoners looked on with greedy eyes as he sat down to feast. Nobody dared come near him.

"Why can't I have what he had?" John asked the guard with the ladle.

"You can if you pay for it," the guard said. "His family's paying a shillin' a day for his keep and protection while he's inside. How much are you getting?"

"Nothing," John said.

The guard shrugged and silently sloshed a ladleful of thin gruel into a wooden bowl and stuck a crust of bread into it. The bread was dotted blue with mould. "Move along."

John's stomach was aching with hunger. He sat down on the ground away from the other prisoners and got

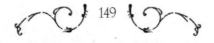

ready to eat the first loathsome mouthful. As he did, a shadow fell across him. It was Jenkins, six-foot four and thick as a barrel.

"I'll have that."

"You've had yours!"

"And now I'm having yours too."

John tried to keep his food, but he had no chance. Jenkins smacked him around the face like a disobedient dog, took his rations and strolled off, munching them. John's eyes burned, but he was damned if he'd cry.

"You could always do what I do when someone gives me grief," said a man called Shaw snidely, settling down beside John.

"What's that?"

"Wait until they're asleep, then cut their throat."

John couldn't tell whether he was joking or not. The eighteen-year-old was being held for murder, after all.

"Or you can just wait for him to die," said Shaw.

John nodded. "They're hanging him on Thursday, I heard."

"Thursday?" Shaw laughed. "He's rotten through with typhus! He won't last that long." The boy pulled his sleeve back and showed John his own sores. "You can't dodge the gaol fever. You'll get 'em too,

150

if you haven't already."

"I've got them," John lied. Then he had a thought. "Maybe they won't put me on the ship, if I'm sick."

"You've got to be joking," Shaw scoffed. "*All* the transportees they load onto them ships are sick, near enough. You know how many survive the journey over? About half! And the ones that make it don't often last more'n a month! They work you 'til you drop, in the colonies."

"But—"

"We're all dead men here," Shaw said, standing up and brushing off his muck-encrusted trousers. "You too. Mummy's not coming to get you."

"But people do return from transportation!" John said. "I've heard stories!"

"Stories," Shaw said, and spat on the ground. The spittle was red with blood. "That's what they are. A load of spit."

"You're lying!"

Shaw looked back at him. "You want to watch it," he said softly. "I've killed men for less."

"He has too," chimed in another young prisoner.

John sat with his head in his hands. They were going to take him thousands of miles away, to a country he

couldn't even imagine. And that was if he didn't die first, from hunger or gaol fever, or Shaw's hands around his neck in the night…

Later that night, as he lay on the meagre planks that were all he had for a bed, he tried to think of his friends, to bring him comfort in this dark place. Beth, especially. Soon, the memory of her face would be all that was left to him. But all he could see was the grotesque, staring-eyed face of the man who had died while he looked on.

He rolled over and opened his eyes. There, revealed in a shaft of bright moonlight, was a symbol scratched into the stone above his bunk. A crude dagger, freshly drawn. It hadn't been there before when he'd tossed and turned trying to get to sleep on previous nights. And as soon as John saw it, he knew he could not sleep at all that night. His life was more directly under threat than he had even imagined.

He recognized that symbol, and it wasn't just a random scrawl – he realized it meant somebody knew that he was a spy. And he couldn't imagine why it mattered, now he was practically a condemned man anyway – but it looked like someone was sending him a threat.

# Chapter Fifteen
## Fatal Complication

Now that Beth had money from Strange, getting into Bridewell to see John was child's play. The guards even escorted her through to a private cell where they could talk without the other prisoners listening in. It wasn't until Beth was halfway down the steps that she realized what they must think she was here for. They probably got a lot of young women in here, paying to visit their sweethearts…

The door closed behind them. "Ten minutes, and that's yer lot," the guard warned through the barred window. "There's rules. And don't try slipping him a file.

We'll be searching him after you've gone."

John looked starved and desperate. He clearly hadn't slept, and the filth of the cells was caked on him like mud. Beth went to hug him anyway, but he held up a warning hand. "Better not. These prison rags are full of lice."

"It's good to see you," she smiled.

"You too," he said, managing a smile in return. "Beth, I have to tell you something—"

"Your family is safe," she told him quickly.

John stared, like a man no longer willing to trust good news. "Safe? How?"

She checked to make sure nobody was eavesdropping, then told him everything: Strange's offer, her decision to accept. She told John about the plan for him to ride out the transportation to America, and that they'd then arrange for him to work as a spy again over there – alongside her and Ralph. And she explained about the advance money she'd negotiated for him. When she told him she'd had some of it passed on to his mother, he slumped in his chair like a weary traveller who finally reaches a resting place, long after he's given up hope of ever finding one.

"God bless you for that," he said. "That makes all of this easier to bear, somehow. Knowing they won't starve,

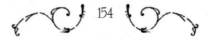

no matter what happens to me."

"Nothing's going to happen to you," Beth chided. "You'll be protected. Strange has it all under control—"

"You're wrong," John said hollowly. "Beth, I'll be a slave in all but name, if I even get there alive. This place is a death trap! Six men died of gaol fever yesterday. *Six!* And there's something else." He lowered his voice even further. "Someone scratched a *dagger* over my bunk."

Beth looked at him, confused for a moment before she realized what he meant. "Dear God," she said. "Vale uses that symbol."

"I know," John said. "An assassin's mark. God alone knows how, but one of Vale's men must be in here with me! I don't know whether he's a prisoner, or a guard, or even one of the governors. But he's going to murder me, and soon. They must have got wind of Strange's plans somehow." He turned pleading eyes upon her. "You have to get me out of here."

Beth nodded, feeling the blood drain from her face. "I'll talk to Strange."

"You'll have to do something fast. Vale's assassin won't strike in the prison, I expect. Too many people watching, too much chance of getting caught, nowhere to hide my body. But once I'm on that transportation ship, he'll finish me for sure. Nothing's easier than getting rid of a body when you're at sea…"

Beth could hear her heart pounding as she rushed to find Ralph. It had only been a couple of hours since she'd seen John, but she'd moved swiftly, and at least now she had a plan, however risky. Strange had been stony-faced but business-like when he'd heard her news, and Beth couldn't help but admire his calm in the face of a crisis. Now she just needed to find Ralph…

She finally located him in an alley round the back of the Pig and Whistle, sitting on a pile of crates like a king holding court. The scruffy children that had surrounded him ducked out of sight when they saw Beth coming.

"It looks like rain," she said casually.

"*Bing avast*, you lot," Ralph ordered, using the secret language only street people knew. He'd taught Beth a few phrases, and she knew "*bing avast*" meant "get out of here". The children obediently fled, darting off down side streets and vaulting over walls into backyards.

"Sorry to interrupt whatever business you were conducting there," Beth said.

"What is it?" He already knew it was an emergency, "it looks like rain" was one of their code phrases.

"One of Vale's assassins is in Bridewell, targeting John," she said. "We can't just let him be transported to America. He'll never survive the journey."

"So what are we going to do?" Ralph said. "Bust him out of prison?"

"You're not far wrong."

Ralph stared. "You can't be serious. How on earth—"

"I'm deadly serious. Strange says the only hope of saving John is to make sure he never gets on that transport ship. He wanted to send some of his men to free him, but I insisted we'd take care of it. This is John we're talking about, after all."

Ralph nodded quickly and blew out a long breath. "Right. Well, where do we start?"

"We need to know everything about the movement of transportees. Where they take them, how they get them there, how many guards they have – *everything*. Can you do that?"

Ralph pursed his lips. "I think so. It'll mean talking to some very nasty people, though." He leaped down from the crate and landed gracefully as a cat. "But I'll ask around. Meet me back here at six."

* * *

Beth wished Ralph had picked a more public meeting place, or at least a better lit one. As she made her way back down the alley, only the light of the moon showed her where to walk. It was almost full now. A shadow up ahead detached itself from the darkness and came towards her. As she braced herself to run or fight, it held its hands up.

"Easy, Beth. It's me."

She let out the breath she'd been holding. "Next time, Ralph, we meet *inside* the pub."

"Nah. Too many nosy parkers." His grin flashed in the dark. "Listen. Here's what I've found out. The prisoners get taken from the Bridewell in batches, still in their chains. They load them onto small boats at Greenwich Harbour, then sail down round the coast to Portsmouth. That's where the transportation ships are, the big 'uns."

"So if we were to set John free, where would we do it?"

"Greenwich," Ralph said quickly. "They have to get 'em onto rowboats and ferry 'em out to the ships, and that's the one time when the chains come off. If we can take down the guards, we can whisk John away before

158

they know what's happened."

Beth's palms ached with excitement. "You think it'll go to plan?"

"I ruddy well hope so, my old duck," Ralph said softly. "Because if we mess this one up and they catch us, it won't just be John who swings for it. We'll be hanging right next to him…"

# Chapter Sixteen

## One Chance

"You have a week to set your affairs in order," Strange told Beth. "I've booked passage to America for yourself, Master Turner and Miss White on the *Antelope*, out of London port."

He clenched his jaw a little when he mentioned Maisie and John, but Beth ignored him. She knew that John's passage on the *Antelope* would be contingent on their rescue going to plan later on, and that Strange wasn't pleased at her insistence that she and Ralph conduct the dangerous snatch-and-grab themselves.

He passed her a smart leather case. "Everything you'll

need for the passage is in here, along with your deeds to the house provided for you in Virginia. Once you are securely in residence, but *not* before, you are to unpick the secret pocket sewn into the lining. It contains the codes and ciphers we will use when communicating."

Beth kept a perfect poker face as she looked over the papers. After living in one room for as long as she could remember, the thought of a whole house made her giddy.

"Naturally you'll need a new identity while you are in America. From the moment you board the *Antelope*, you are no longer Beth Johnson. You are Lady Johanna Easton, late of Oxford, travelling to assume control of the estate left to you by your deceased uncle. Miss White is to be your maidservant, Maisie Blanchet. Turner will become your manservant, John Briskell—" He stopped and glowered at her before continuing. "That is, if you succeed in freeing him, of course, and do not get yourself captured in the process…"

"We will succeed," Beth replied confidently. "And in any case, if I'm to run my own spy ring in America, it's as well we all start trusting my judgment." She arched an eyebrow, and Strange let out a short sigh. "Actually," she continued, "I had a thought. Won't a noble English heiress attract a lot of attention in the colonies?"

"Consider it 'hiding in plain sight'," Strange said, as if he were rather proud of the idea.

"So, what if any genuine blue-bloods happen to meet me? What if I eat my quince with the wrong fork or something, and blow the whole show?"

"I'm sure your acting talents are up to the challenge," Strange said stiffly. "If there's anything you're unsure of, research it. Once you are established in America, your priority, of course, must be to locate Vale. Begin your search in Jamestown. As the first port of call for most British subjects, it seems the likeliest place to run him to ground."

At his invitation, Beth opened up the packing crate and took a look at the costumes Strange had had made.

"Goodness," she breathed. There was an entire ladies' ensemble, from the corsetry to the fans, along with combs, make-up and even perfumes. Alongside those were maids' outfits for Maisie and smart coats and wigs for John. The cost must have been tremendous. There was more money enclosed with the documents, she saw, in a purse marked "expenses". Strange was clearly wagering a fortune on her success. She thought of the risk she would be courting by breaking John out, and her stomach did a flip-flop. If she were arrested, all this

planning would be wrecked beyond hope of salvation.

She leafed through the documents again, feeling like she was preparing for the most important role she would ever play. Many of them were letters from a "Carstairs", explaining to Lady Easton what her new position would entail.

"Carstairs is your family lawyer, and a trusted friend," Strange explained. "That's to be my identity in our correspondence. You will write to me once a week. Use the pinprick method to spell out your coded messages."

Once a week seemed like a lot. "What should I write about?"

"Use your imagination. I'm sure you can come up with many reasons why a young girl would be asking her mentor for guidance."

Yes, Beth reflected, there would be a lot of improvization to come, and very soon, a rather complicated conversation with Maisie to be had. Plus somehow she had to transform herself from a London actress into a fine lady, with only seven days to rehearse. But there was an even *more* urgent problem to take care of first...

\* \* \*

The transportation ships waited silently out on the middle of the Thames, where the water was deepest. The guards gathered at the railings looked bored. They had no idea that Ralph and Beth were hiding out of sight beneath the nearby landing pier. The two of them crouched on a patch of river bank exposed by the retreating tide, mere feet from the water's edge.

They had arrived over an hour ago, when the sun was setting. Now it was long after dark, and Beth's feet were freezing. The wet river-bank mud sucked at them greedily. Ralph, ever practical, had smeared some of it on their faces to help disguise them, and they had also tied old scarves round their mouths and noses, so they now looked like highwaymen who'd been wrestling in the dirt. Ralph was all but invisible next to her; only the slow sound of his breathing revealed that he was there at all.

"So many guards," she whispered. "Ralph, tell me this isn't crazy."

"Wish I could," Ralph said. "It ain't the guards on the ships we've got to worry about, though. They can't reach us. It's the ones on the shore that's the problem."

"How many of them are there?"

"We won't know until they turn up."

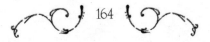

"And you're sure this is the best chance we've got?"

"It's the *only* chance. They'll have to take the prisoners' chains off to get 'em in the jolly-boats. Once they're in the convict ship, they'll be straight back in irons again."

Now that she had seen where their rescue attempt would happen, Beth was more anxious than ever. A set of wooden steps descended from the landing pier down to the water and vanished under the surface. That was where the boats would take the prisoners on board. She and Ralph would have to wade into the water to reach John. She prayed it wasn't deep.

"Hear that?" Ralph hissed suddenly.

Beth could hardly miss it. It was the sound of a crowd of people arriving at the harbour, first in dribs and drabs, then in dozens. She'd heard passers-by up above ever since they'd begun their vigil, but this hubbub was new and loud. A creak of wagon wheels in the distance, a clatter of hooves … something was happening.

"It's them!" she whispered. She craned her head round a post to peer up at the dockside. All along the harbour, people had gathered. Many of the women were crying, and the men were mostly shouting at the top of their voices, calling out names: "Timmy!" "Ben!" "Jacko!"

Then the first of the prison carts came into view.

The cart's high wheels meant Beth got a good clear look at the ragged figures sat together there, bumping over the dockside cobbles a good head and shoulders above the crowd. Her heart in her mouth, she looked from face to miserable face – but none of them was John.

The screaming and howling from the crowd reached a frenzy. "My boy!" one woman screamed. "He's innocent, he never done no wrong, let him go!" For a horrible second, Beth thought it was Mrs Turner; but then she saw the guard elbow the woman, knocking her away from the cart. It wasn't her, but another poor mother watching her son being torn away.

"Looks like there's guards on every cart," Ralph whispered. "This ain't going to be easy."

"They're bringing them aboard," Beth whispered back. "Let's get back under cover. We need to see this!"

Footsteps tramped on the boards above, echoingly loud. With them came a rattling cacophony as the prisoners' chains were dragged down the length of the landing pier behind them. Ralph and Beth froze as the first of the convict ships let down its jolly-boat – a long rowboat used to ferry passengers between ship and shore. Two guards rowed it across the water until it came to rest alongside the steps, and a rope was tossed up and made fast to a mooring pole.

There was a metallic bang and a rattle, a guard gave a gruff order, and the first of the prisoners came tottering down the steps without his chains. He looked around nervously, as if considering a desperate last-minute escape.

"Get in!" barked the guard on the boat, reaching for the cudgel that hung from his belt. Cowed, the prisoner obeyed. The guard tied his hands with a rope, knotted it tightly and forced him to sit down. Another followed, then another, until the boat lay low in the water with the weight of so many men. Beth stared in horror and pity as the guards began to row, bearing the convicts across the river to the waiting ships.

"Why don't they just keep the chains on?" she whispered.

"Because they're heavy, and if the transportees fall in and drown, nobody gets paid to ship 'em to America," said Ralph bitterly. "And because them chains are the property of Bridewell Prison, to be sent back ready for the next load."

The boat was halfway to the ship when shouting broke out. One of the prisoners had stood up and was yelling. "Farewell, dear London!" he cried.

"Remember old Jacko!"

The guard cut his speech short with a blow to the back of the head and the man collapsed. A roar of anger went up from the crowd at the harbour.

"God, a riot's all we need," Ralph whispered. "Let's hope nobody else gets the urge to give a speech!"

"Can you blame them? They're leaving their homes and families! They'll probably never see them again."

Beth felt sick at the way the prisoners were being treated. They might be criminals, but they weren't animals. This wasn't the England she'd fought to protect.

For the next half hour they waited, the cries of miserable people ringing in their ears. Families wept and guards dragged women back from the cartloads of condemned men, refusing to grant a final kiss no matter how much screaming and fainting went on.

"They really *are* going to have a riot on their hands if they keep this up," Ralph murmured. "I had no idea it was this bad."

Beth shuddered. A riot would mean the Watch coming down in force, and no chance of ever saving John.

Right at that moment, she saw him. His chains must have just been struck off, because he was reluctantly descending the steps towards the waiting boat. His head

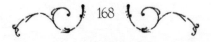

was bowed in total defeat.

"Wait for it," Ralph told her. "Got to time this just right…"

"Move!" barked the guard from above them. John increased his pace by the tiniest degree, moving in a slow trudge like the condemned man he was. When he reached the bottom step he raised his head and looked around, as if to check for certain that no rescue was coming after all.

"Now!" Ralph cried.

Together they sprinted down from their hiding place, running alongside the pier supports and splashing out into the ice-cold river. John looked around, and his eyes widened as he suddenly realized what he was seeing.

"Come on!" Beth shouted. The water was up to her thighs, soaking her skirts, adding dangerous weight. Hell with it – she'd tear them off if she had to. John leaped down from the platform and landed in waist-high water.

The splash seemed to burst open the floodgates of total chaos. The prisoners already in the boat stood up and began shouting encouragement, the crowd at the harbour hollered, and the guards all around shouted orders at one another. A dog barked loudly and someone blew on a whistle.

John came wading quickly towards Beth. He held his hand out to her, and she reached out to him. Their hands clasped, but the next moment, there was a second splash. One of the guards had followed John into the river, cudgel raised. "Get back here!" he yelled.

Ralph stepped into his path and lashed out with the speed of a born street fighter. His fist struck the guard's jaw with a sound like cracking nuts, and the man toppled back against the wooden steps.

"Run!" Beth shouted.

Pulling John behind her, she sprinted along the muddy river bank, making for the stone quayside steps she knew were only a few dozen yards away. Ralph ran to catch up with them, cursing. Pinpoint flashes of fire came from the prison ships, and something exploded with a sharp crack just beside Beth's head.

"They're firing muskets!" Ralph yelled. "Run, for God's sake!"

They scrambled up the wet stone steps, with the yelling guards close on their heels. But the dockside crowds were surging in now, desperate to see what was going on. Beth suddenly felt a spark of hope – if they could just break through the crowds, they would shake the guards off!

John's hand was still locked tight in hers. She wouldn't let him go, not now, not ever. Without looking back, she plunged into the mass of people swarming at the top of the steps. Hands clutched at her, faces loomed in front of her, and all around was shouting and screaming. A fresh rattle of musket fire came from the ships; there was a shriek, but she couldn't look to see who'd been hit. She kept going, pushing between the bodies, ignoring the noise.

Then they were out, running into the shadowed labyrinth of the London streets. A fierce joy seized Beth as she led John and Ralph down a side alley she knew, then through the backyard of an ancient tavern and a cooper's forecourt before rejoining the main road. She might be a muddy and bedraggled, but this was her territory and she knew it better than anyone.

On and on they ran, until the pain in Beth's side was like an open wound and her breaths came ragged and shallow. Only when the three of them were deep into Deptford, and Ralph was trying to tell her between wheezing gasps that the guards had long since been shaken off, did they stop.

Even then she still held John's hand in the darkness, defying anyone to snatch him away from her again.

# Chapter Seventeen

## May the Circle Be Unbroken

Beth sat by herself in the back of the tavern, anxiously watching over the three plates of food she'd paid for. She was starting to get odd looks from the other patrons. Why were Ralph and John taking so long? When they finally arrived, she understood.

"You look like a new man," she whispered to John.

"I wish I felt like one," John said with a weak smile. He was no longer wearing the shabby grey prison clothes he'd escaped in. Instead, he wore a baggy shirt tucked into an old pair of sailor's breeches. His hair was soaking wet.

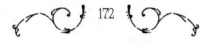

"Told you I'd thought of everything," Ralph grinned, sitting down. "You should have seen him changing into my old clothes in that alley! We'd have been in a right pickle if the guards had come, me with an armful of prison rags, him with the moonlight shining off his bare—"

Beth choked. "Ralph, that's quite enough!"

"And you know what?" Ralph went on, undaunted. "He's such a proper little gentleman, he wouldn't come back to meet you here until he'd been and had a wash at a water pipe."

"I've never been so dirty in my life as I was in that place," John muttered. He scratched himself. "I don't feel like I'll ever be clean again."

"Prison dirt finds its way into all sorts of places," Ralph admitted.

"Be honest, Beth. I'm still filthy, aren't I?"

"Well…"

"Come on. We're moving over there." John picked up his plate and moved to the darkest corner of the inn, where nobody could see them. Beth and Ralph sighed and went to join him.

Now he could finally feel safe, John ate like a famished wolf, forgetting his usual manners in his haste to cram

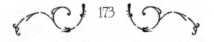

food into his mouth. Beth noticed him touching his ankle from time to time, as if he wanted to make sure of something. He saw her noticing and blushed.

"I can still feel those chains," he said. "I know they're gone, but it's like they're haunting me."

"We'll never let them do that to you again," Beth promised.

John looked down. "I can take care of myself, you know."

"She only means we'll be watching out for one another, once we're set up in America," Ralph said through a mouthful of his own food.

"I don't mean to sound ungrateful, of course—" John began, but Beth waved him off.

"I can't wait to get going," she said excitedly. "Now I know we're all going, and Maisie too, I just wish we could be in America *now*!"

"Getting through this week is going to be the real trick," Ralph said, sounding like he didn't want to count any chickens. "Don't forget we're harbouring an escaped fugitive here. John's going to have the law breathing down his neck as well as Vale's hatchet man, whoever he is." He turned to John. "Don't suppose you have any more of an idea who Vale's assassin might be?"

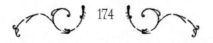

"No idea at all," John sighed. "All the time I was in the prison, even when we were in the carts going to the transport ship, I kept looking over my shoulder. I was sure the assassin was going to make a move. But nothing happened." He sagged in his chair. "I can't believe I'm out of that death trap at last! Good God, I need to sleep. I haven't slept in three days."

"You'd better doss down with me this week," Ralph offered. "You can't go back to your family's house. That's the first place the assassin will look."

John stiffened. "If he hurts my family—"

"That won't happen," Beth said sternly, laying a gentle hand on his knee. "Vale wouldn't gain anything by it, would he?"

"I'm not going to get a chance to say goodbye to them, am I?" John said, the truth of it hitting home like a hammer. "It ... it might be years before I see them again."

"They're safe and they have money, and you're alive," Beth said firmly. "I made sure Strange got word to them that you are all right. You have to keep that in your mind."

John nodded and smiled gratefully at her.

Ralph cleared his throat. "And if it comes to it, you

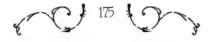

could always just stay here in London. Strange can't force you to come to America with us, can he? He could sort you out with a new identity."

"No," John said. "I do want to come. You're right - my family will be OK. And London's turned sour on me," he said with a wry smile. "Plague, hunger, stupid bloody beadles acting like a law unto themselves – give me the land of liberty any day!"

Beth smiled. "And we'll still be getting a chance to serve King and Country by getting to that criminal Vale."

"I'll drink to that," Ralph said, raising his tankard.

But Beth was quietly a little saddened at John's bitterness. It was as if prison had eaten away what was left of the wide-eyed boy in him, leaving behind a hardened young man. She decided to lighten the mood.

"Did I mention that you'll be playing the role of my manservant, John?" she said with a grin.

John looked to Ralph. "Mind giving me a reference?" he joked.

Ralph scratched his chin and thought. "Having worked with this young man on many occasions, I can vouch for his high moral character," he said solemnly. "However, he does often end up in trouble. He badly needs guidance to him on the correct path, like. Just as

well I'll be coming with him, ain't it?"

"But I never did ask – what's *your* cover story going to be, Ralph?" Beth asked. "I can't have two manservants, can I?"

"It's a sailor's life for me," Ralph said with a grin. "Strange sorted me out a position on board the *Antelope*, as a junior seaman."

"You're coming on the very same ship as us?" Beth asked, pleased. She knew Ralph had been to sea before – even, once, on a pirate ship!

"'Course I am. What, you didn't think I was going to wait around when the rest of you were shipping out, did you?" Ralph tutted. "As if you could get rid of me that easy."

They all smiled at one another. Their spy ring would remain unbroken after all. Now they just had to wait to cast off for a new world.

# Chapter Eighteen
## Adieu, Adieu

"I can't believe how quickly this week has gone by," Beth said.

She and Maisie were standing together at the window of their bare room, watching the street for signs of their carriage. Hiring it in advance had been expensive, but Beth hadn't had any other choice; walking to the *Antelope* would have been quite out of the question for a high-born lady and her maid. So there was nothing to do now but enjoy the experience.

Beth was quite pleased with the cover story she'd dreamed up. Naturally Maisie couldn't be told the

truth – that Beth, John and Ralph were all spies travelling undercover – so instead, Beth had spun a tale around a wealthy, eccentric theatre patron. This peculiar and rather paranoid old man, she said, had property and land in America that he wanted Beth to keep a watchful eye on, and he'd come up with the ruse of disguising her as a highborn lady along with her staff, knowing that she was a good enough actress to pull it off. And, Beth told her friend, he was paying her a small fortune to do so. *Layers upon layers*, Beth thought; *lies piled upon lies.* She felt uncomfortable deceiving Maisie, even if it did mean they got to travel together to America. However, Maisie didn't baulk at the story one bit. Beth had barely finished telling it before she had begun to pull on her maid's outfit.

Now the girl couldn't keep still. "When's our carriage coming?" she said, for the umpteenth time. "Oh, this is all so exciting!"

Beth smiled. Maisie might not be completing her current role at the theatre, but she certainly enjoyed playing a role! And she'd been a glorious success during the week when she had taken to the stage as Maid Marian and the patrons of London had cheered and cheered at the sound of the young girl's beautiful voice, enough

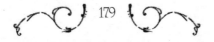

for William Huntingdon to genuinely want the girl to join the company for future productions. He'd been saddened to have to find another actress to take over the role of Marian for the last few performances, as Maisie had supposedly "strained her inexperienced voice".

But now the girl was as excited as she had been on her first night on the stage. When there had been a knock on the door ten minutes ago, Maisie had practically jumped out of her skin, but it had only been a messenger delivering a note from Ralph, to say he'd had word from his contacts and there was not even a whisper of Vale's assassin anywhere. Beth wondered whether the shadowy would-be killer had given up the hunt, or was just biding his time.

Leaving Maisie to watch, she took a last look around their little room. It was strange to see it stripped bare of all her familiar things. Her clothes and possessions, along with the vast collection of outfits Strange had provided, were already on their way to the *Antelope*. Her manservant, John Briskell, had seen to that.

And an efficient servant Briskell was, Beth thought with a grin. It was astonishing how smart he looked in his white wig and fancy jacket, and how politely he answered his lady employer. Nobody would have guessed

that he was really John *Turner*, or that his ankle still bore a red weal where his prison chains had chafed him raw. Maisie was happy with Beth's explanation that he'd had a last-minute reprieve from his sentence, and was also using this cover story as a far less dangerous passage to a new life in America.

"Let's do a final rehearsal," Beth suggested. "So, Miss Blanchet, remind me how we spent this morning?"

"First I fetched you the water to make your ablutions, m'lady," Maisie said. "Then I dressed you, and arranged your hair just so."

"And a marvellous job you did," Beth said. "And then?"

Maisie frowned, then remembered. "You went down to breakfast and I tidied the room. I cleaned all your brushes and combs, and folded away your things, and organized your jewellery. A shocking state it was in too, if I may say so, ma'am."

"I don't know what I'd do without you, Miss Blanchet," Beth laughed.

"Tell you what, it's a good job I'm only pretending to do all this stuff," Maisie said. "Imagine if I really did have to clean up after you all the time. I'd have a fit!"

"You'd better not tease me like that in public,"

Beth said with a grin.

"Yes, ma'am," Maisie sighed. "I know the rules. 'A lady's maid is always respectful and obedient, even if the lady is throwing a tantrum and breaking the china.'"

"I promise I won't make it hard for you. Though we should probably have a couple of Lady Frightful scenes, just to make it look real."

"Lady Frightful!" Maisie shuddered, remembering.

To research their roles, Maisie and Beth had gone to all the places they could think of where ladies and their maids would be, so they could watch how they behaved. Lady Frightful was the name they gave to a ghastly woman in a coffee shop, with hair "all done up like a bird's nest" as Maisie had observed, and a terrified cowering maidservant.

Every other word out of Lady Frightful's mouth had been "stupid". The stupid girl had failed to do this or that, had brought cold water instead of hot, had broken a mirror, had lost – or stolen – an earring.

"If she was my boss, I'd smother her in her sleep," Maisie had muttered.

But other ladies had provided better examples, and soon Beth had been practising the finer points in front of her mirror: the demure peek out from behind a fan, the

offering of one's hand for a gentleman to kiss, the slight lifting of the skirts as she swept into a room. She read guides to table etiquette and looked up the names of lords and barons she ought to have heard of, along with descriptions of their estates and houses. By the end of it all, they both felt ready to put on a good show for their fellow passengers.

Then came the only sad part, saying their goodbyes to Big Moll, to all their friends at the theatre … that had all been mercifully quick, and necessarily a little woolly on details.

"The carriage is here!" Maisie squeaked at last.

"Very well. From this moment on we're Lady Easton and Maisie Blanchet," Beth said. "We can't be Beth and Maisie again until we're on our own."

"I understand."

Beth quickly kissed her cheek. "Good luck."

"You too!" Maisie ran downstairs to open the door for Beth as if she were born to it.

The carriage driver didn't bat an eyelid at the sight of a grand lady descending the steps of the Peacock and Pie. He touched the brim of his hat and said, "Where to, ma'am?"

"Hay's Wharf, my good man." Beth swept majestically

aboard, holding her embroidered skirts carefully aside as she stepped up. Maisie, carrying her small bag, climbed up to take her place beside the driver. With a lurch, they were off.

"So far, so good," Beth whispered to herself.

The *Antelope* was an English galleon, standing proud on the water. The young manservant waiting on the quayside looked every bit as proud to be sailing on her. Beth smiled to herself. John did love his ships. He looked like he was posing for a dramatic portrait, like Sir Francis Drake.

She put the smile away and assumed an expression of frosty calm as she descended from her carriage. "Good morning, Briskell."

"M'lady," John said, with a bow. "Your belongings have been stowed aboard and I'm told your cabin is ready."

"Very good."

"Captain Clark requests the pleasure of your company at his table tonight."

"Please tell our captain I shall be glad to join him,"

Beth replied. All the "quality" passengers on a voyage of this sort could be expected to dine with the captain, as a mark of his respect for their status.

She hesitated before stepping onto the gangplank and gave the ship a look over. This would be their home for many months to come. Even for a grand lady, it would surely be uncomfortable, possibly even dangerous. Her life was in the sailors' hands now. One of those sailors was waving to her, high aloft in the rigging, and she realized with a small smile that it was Ralph, sporting a fine new rigger's uniform. She gave him the tiniest of waves back and then strode on board, with Maisie trotting behind like an excited puppy.

The captain himself, a beaming bewhiskered man, showed Beth to her cabin. She almost felt sorry for deceiving him, he was so eager to please. "Now, I'm right across the corridor from you, Lady Easton," he kept saying, "so don't hesitate to knock if you need me, day or night."

"I shall."

"And if any of the crew are uncivil to you, pray tell me so. I'll have 'em flogged!"

"Uh, thank you for your gallantry, Captain Clark," Beth said with a curtsey, and Clark's cheeks positively

glowed with satisfaction. After the captain's ready talk of flogging his crew over what might be simply the word of a passenger, Beth no longer felt the slightest bit sorry about her deceit. Instead, she decided to exploit his feelings to the hilt. She opened the door onto a cabin almost as big as their old room in the Peacock and Pie. A washstand and dresser had been provided, and a sumptuous bed stood against one side, with a plainer one at its foot. It even had a port-hole offering a view of the ocean.

"What luxury," was all Maisie could say.

"Indeed," Beth breathed, once the captain was out of earshot.

Soon after, the call came from below: "Weigh anchor!"

The great ship began to move, and passengers crowded to the railing to wave their final goodbyes. Ralph worked his way along the deck, and paused alongside Beth for a moment. "Bye, London," he muttered at the passing skyline. "Truth is, you're just too small for me."

Beth's mind was racing with thoughts of her new life. A big house, a theatrical company of her own, and the spy work. She'd be on unfamiliar territory. There would

be dangers in America she'd never faced before. Vale was there already, with a head start on her. She could only guess at what layers of protection he might have built up around himself. But she was Strange's trusted agent – not a running dog, as Vale had contemptuously dismissed her, but a cunning, ruthless hunter. She'd run him to ground.

"I'm coming home," Maisie said happily. "America's where I really belong. And my father's there, looking for me with his eyes as blue as the ocean."

John was watching by her side as well.

"Goodbye, London," Beth heard him whisper, so low only she could hear. "Goodbye, prison and poverty and hunger. Hello, America, land of opportunity … and freedom."

# Chapter Nineteen

## The Captain's Table

"How can it be dinner time already?" Beth protested, flapping her hands. "It feels like we just set off!"

"Hold still!" Maisie told her, wrestling her hair into place and securing it with a final comb. "I knew we should have practised this more."

"I don't even know who the other high-class passengers are," Beth lamented. "I should have asked Strange to look into it."

"You'll do fine," Maisie said. "There. You look wonderful."

Beth sighed. "I wish we could eat together, but …

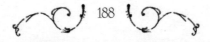

you know."

"Servants don't eat with the gentry. I know me place, m'lady," her friend said with a grin.

Beth hurried up to the captain's mess, where the rest of the guests were already sat at table. To her horror, she saw none of them had started their meal. They were all clearly waiting indignantly for her.

"I'm sorry to be so late," she stammered.

"Not at all!" Captain Clark said, ushering her to her place. She went to pull her chair back and sit, then caught herself just in time. A lady didn't seat herself; she waited for a gentleman to do it. Sure enough, Captain Clark pulled out the chair, and she settled on it in a rustle of skirts, graceful as a swan. *That was close*, she thought.

After three courses and only a small amount of embarrassment when Beth tried to open an oyster with a fruit knife, it was time for the traditional after-dinner toasts. Beth was glad to finally be reaching the end of the arduous meal and patronizing conversation.

"Here's a health to His Majesty!" said Captain Clark, standing up. Everyone drank.

"Long may he reign over England, and all her colonies too," said Hardwicke, an elderly passenger with a Naval background.

Another passenger, a flabby man called Howell, took exception to those words.

"Try telling them that when we reach Virginia!" he said scornfully. "The way some of them talk, they'd just as soon throw off His Majesty and turn rebel!"

"Stuff and nonsense," Hardwicke retorted. "That's just a few malcontents, stirring up trouble. We've guns enough to keep 'em in line."

"It may have just been a few at first, but the rot's well and truly set in by now," Howell insisted.

"I've heard such guff before. We're the mightiest empire the world has ever seen, and yet you talk as if we're on the verge of collapse!"

Beth listened as the argument grew heated, but kept her mouth firmly shut and tried not to look too interested. Her role in this was to sit and look pretty while the gentlemen talked. She couldn't help the thoughts churning in her mind, however. America was supposed to be loyal to her parent country, just like a daughter to her mother. The English had worked hard for many years to colonize the place, so why shouldn't the colonists love their King?

An uneasy suspicion slowly surfaced in her mind. There was one person who lived to stir up hatred of the

King wherever he went: Vale. Could he be embroiled in this somehow? Maybe she should investigate some of those "malcontents" when she reached America…

Meanwhile, John was settling in to his own cabin. It was half the size of Beth's, and his bunk was one of four. A colossal Yorkshireman, already lying in one of the bunks, raised an eyebrow at him as he unpacked. "You'd better not be a snorer," the man warned. "Shared a cabin with a snorer once. Had to drown him." John froze, still on edge from prison, but the man's wink relaxed him a little.

There was barely room to move in the cabin once the other passengers arrived. As well as the Yorkshire giant, John was packed in with a gunsmith called Briggs and an Irish seaman called Murdoch, who seemed to have visited every country on Earth.

"First crossing?" Briggs asked him, offering a swig of gin from a flask, which John declined. "Don't be nervous. Our captain's hard, but seasoned. We'll reach Virginia in one piece."

"He's a fine man is Clark," said Murdoch. "Some of these dogs who set to sea, they haven't a clue how to sail.

191

All they care about is the money."

"That lady of yours isn't shy of a few bob, is she?" said Briggs. "You landed on your feet with that one, son."

"Lady Easton is an angel," John said firmly. "Her family took me in when I was small. I've served them ever since."

"No disrespect intended, I swear!" Briggs shook John's hand and looked genuinely sorry. "This lad's a proper old-fashioned servant, isn't he? Won't hear his lady's name taken lightly, even in jest. It's not just a job for you, is it, being in service?"

John shook his head and stayed modestly silent.

"There you go. 'Well done, thou good and faithful servant.' Good fortune to you and your good lady!"

Briggs drank again, and John smiled inwardly. The man was doing a splendid job of convincing the other passengers that John really was a servant. Over a meal of fresh meat and bread – the last they'd get for a long time – John's fellow passengers traded stories of the New World. They'd all made good money there and couldn't wait to return.

"I tell you, lad, it's a place of freedom for the working man," Murdoch said, thumping the boards to drive his point home. "All the hard work gets left to the slaves and

the convicts. If you've a tradesman's skill or two, you can make a mint."

"And if you don't, you can learn," Briggs pointed out. "Tradesmen over there are always looking for apprentices. As it happens, I'm looking for a smart young fella to teach my trade to."

"Save your breath," said the Yorkshireman. "Johnny here'll be in service 'til the day he dies, waiting on his lady's pleasure." He gave John another wink.

"So America really is a land of freedom?" John asked innocently.

"Well, yes and no," said Murdoch. "The slaves don't do too well out of it, truth be told. Nor do them Quakers."

"I've heard of them." Quakers were a peaceful religious sect, from what John had been told. "Why would anyone take against them?"

"That's not for me to say," Murdoch said with a dark look. "But there's been a Quaker woman hanged, and she won't be the first." He paused. "You're not a Quaker, are you, lad?"

"No, I'm not!" John said. *But if anyone over there finds out what I really am*, he thought, *I'd be hanged too…*

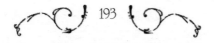

# Chapter Twenty

## Confrontation

Over the next few days, John and Ralph met one another by chance and play-acted the beginnings of a friendship, but it wasn't until they were a week out to sea that John finally had a chance to catch up with Ralph properly, down by the crew quarters. He was swigging water from a tin cup, taking a rare break from his duties.

"Sea air must be doing you good," John said. "You look healthier than I've ever seen you."

"It's all them nutritious weevils in the ship's biscuits," Ralph grinned. "That and the hard work. You forget what a slog it is when you're on land." He lowered his

voice. "How's you-know-who?"

"She's well," John said. Ralph nodded. That was all they needed to say on the matter. One of the other sailors squeezed past them and they made small talk until the man was out of the way.

"Keep it under your hat," Ralph murmured as he looked back at the man, "but some of my new chums on the crew have got their fingers into a very juicy pie indeed."

"Go on."

"There's boxes and packets being brought on board that ain't on any cargo lists. When we stopped at Portsmouth, a fair few people earned a lot of extra cash smuggling them things on board."

"For whom?"

"Private customers. Well, *one* private customer, at least. Sounds like it might be someone we both know, don't it? Could be ammunition, documents to do with his plotting…"

"If these boxes aren't on the cargo lists," John wondered, "where are your 'chums' stowing them?"

"That's what I'd like to find out," Ralph said. "But I don't think I'm going to. There's no more stops until we reach Virginia, so there's no new boxes to load and

nothing to cut me in on."

"I'll pass that on to you-know-who. And we should have a look round," John suggested. "Next chance we get." He fell silent as yet another sailor entered the narrow passageway. The young man turned sideways to pass them and, for a second, looked right into John's face.

"Haven't you learned to keep your nose out of other people's business yet?" the sailor said.

"I beg your pardon?" John stammered.

"No more games. It's you. I know you, Turner. And you know me. Or you ought to."

"I sincerely doubt it…"

But the words died away as he said them. To his mounting horror, he realized he *did* know the young man. The sailor saw the look in his eyes and grinned wolfishly. It was Shaw.

"The last time I saw your face we were in Bridewell, prisoners both," Shaw said with relish. "We have some unfinished business to attend to. I was let off of my sentence before I could take care of you, but isn't it lucky our paths have crossed again?"

"I've never seen you before in my life," John protested, hoping he sounded adamant.

"Do you know the penalty for *escaping* from prison,

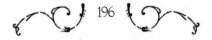

196

Turner?" Shaw continued softly, ignoring him. "*Hanging.* I'm sure the captain will be very interested to know he's got a fugitive on board his ship." He leaned in and whispered "He'll do my work for me. Nice. I won't even have to get my hands bloody."

"How dare you accuse me of being a criminal!" John burst out. "I've been a servant all of my life, in service to the Easton family of Oxford! Now, if you'll excuse me, her ladyship has need of me." He shoved past and headed for the upper deck, not stopping to listen to anything else that came out of Shaw's mouth.

Beth looked up, startled, as John slipped into her cabin. He pressed his back to the door. "Can we talk in private?"

"Miss Blanchet, kindly fetch Briskell a brandy," Beth told Maisie. "He looks like he could use one."

As Maisie left the room, John sat down heavily on the bed. "It's him, Beth," he said. "Vale's assassin. It's one of the sailors. I'd known him in Bridewell, he's named Shaw. He's not in London. He's here!"

"Oh no," Beth said, turning pale. "Did he recognize you?"

197

John nodded. Waves of sickness and fear washed over him. "He's going to tell the captain who I am. He'll have me hanged, do his dirty work for him. And once the captain finds out who *I* am, he'll get suspicious. He might uncover who *you* are. I can't let that happen. I'd sooner die, Beth! I'll throw myself overboard, make it look like an accident—"

Beth grabbed him by the shoulders. "Calm down. Right now." She leaned in and whispered, "We need to stay in character, no matter what. Don't call me Beth again."

"What are we going to do?" John said, taking several deep breaths to steady himself. Beth sat down at her dressing table and opened an ornate make-up box. She opened a pot of powder.

"You are not to throw yourself overboard, for a start."

"All right."

There was silence for a moment as Beth applied lavish make-up, turning her skin porcelain-white and making her lips into a Cupid's bow of dark blood-red. John watched her, dumbfounded. Maisie came back, bringing the brandy, and handed it to him. He sipped it gratefully.

"What are you doing?" John eventually asked.

"We have a lot of improvizing to do in the next ten

minutes," Beth told him. "I'm going to need you to act your heart out. Can you do that for me?"

"I'll do my best."

"Good. We are going to make a scene, and everyone on this ship needs to see it. Miss Blanchet, I'll need you to cower fearfully when you see me raging at Briskell." Beth patted rouge onto her cheeks. "It's time to bring Lady Frightful out of her box."

Maisie nodded in perfect comprehension, and smiled. "Very good, ma'am."

"Here's what we'll say. Listen carefully, both of you. We aren't going to get a chance to rehearse this…"

Shaw was back at work, scrubbing the deck down on his hands and knees. This had all worked out perfectly. Vale would pay a handsome sum for Turner's death, and he'd be impressed with the clever way Shaw had used the captain to make it happen. He might even get a promotion…

He yelped as a china plate smashed on the boards right in front of him. Fragments went zinging over the edge of the deck and into the sea. He drew himself up, just in time to see Turner go racing past and come to a cringing halt against the railings.

"I'm sorry, m'lady!" he whimpered.

Shaw turned in amazement to see the lady that Turner had been serving, standing like a Gorgon on the other side of him. She held a second plate in her hand, ready to fling.

"'Sorry' is not good enough, Briskell!" Beth declared, using the most strident upper-class tones she could manage. "I shall not tolerate your slackness for one second longer!"

"It shan't happen again, I swear." John was doing a fantastic job of seeming terrified.

"When I instruct you to bring me my morning water at seven, I expect it to be brought at seven sharp, and not at your leisure," she said in a clipped voice. What would Lady Frightful say, she wondered? Ah, yes, of course. "*Stupid* boy."

Now came the crucial part; feeding the gathering audience John's fake history. Shaw had a first-class seat to this performance. He was watching open-mouthed, and sailors from all over the ship were staring at her. But John wasn't saying anything. He was just cowering in pretend fear, and beginning to look like a bit of a ham.

Beth had to start talking again:

"I don't know where this slothfulness comes from, Briskell," she snapped. "Your poor mother had none of it, God rest her soul! She served my family admirably every day of her life. Do you think that just because you were born under our roof and grew up in our service, you can take liberties? Is that it?"

John still didn't seem sure what to say next. He glanced over and saw Ralph, who gave him an encouraging nod.

"I just got caught up talking to some of the sailors," he whined.

Beth seized on the opportunity. "Pah! You and your obsession with the sea! Even when you were a little boy, you were always playing with toy boats!" She pointed to the doorway that led to the cabins. "Get in there, do the work you're paid to do, and if I hear any more impertinence from you I shall ask Captain Clark to have you whipped!"

John hurried back inside, hunching his shoulders as if Beth might fling the second plate at him after all. Beth lifted her skirts to leave, then stopped and looked around at the crew, who by now were all watching her to see what she'd do next.

"What are you all gawping at?" she demanded.

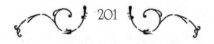

Instantly they went back to work, giving one another meaningful looks. Beth stormed off to her cabin, slammed the door shut behind her and collapsed into John's arms, stifling her laughter.

"If that didn't do it," John whispered, "nothing will."

"Shaw won't dare accuse you of being John Turner now," Beth agreed. "It's his word against mine."

"You're a genius. A common sailor wouldn't dare call a grand lady a liar, would he?"

Beth smiled secretively. "Oh, I think Captain Clark might have something to say about it if he did. He's a cruel man, but he does have his uses!"

# Chapter Twenty-One

**Lost at Sea**

Three weeks had passed since the *Antelope* set sail, and with fair winds and calm seas, she was making good progress. Nothing more had come of Shaw's threats towards John, which was a relief to Beth, John and Ralph.

But the sailors were muttering ominously when they saw the thunderheads gathering in the west; and sure enough, that night the rain came lashing down like volleys of lead shot. On the heels of the rain came the wind, and the sea, woken from its calm slumber, reared up like a wild animal and began to toss the ship to and

fro on its back. Soon, despite the late hour, not a sailor on board could be spared. Hammocks swung empty in the crew quarters as the first mate yelled out the orders that the sailors scrambled to obey. Hatches were secured, loose objects lashed in place, and sails furled in the hope that the storm's fury would quickly pass.

Beth woke up at the sound of a cup smashing. She sat up in bed and saw all the loose things on her dresser sliding first to one side, then to the other as the ship rolled and pitched. Maisie's bed was empty. The unlatched cabin door swung to and fro with the ship.

Still in her nightdress, Beth went to the window and gasped out loud in fear. The horizon was all wrong. She saw tremendous hills of black water surge past, topped with white foam. Next second, she heard the juddering crash as a fresh wave hammered the ship. The panicked shouts of passengers rang out from the other cabins.

Maisie appeared at the doorway, holding onto the doorframe to steady her.

"Storm's getting worse, miss!" she yelled. "We need to lash ourselves in!"

"What?" Beth shouted back.

"I talked to the other passengers, the ones who've made the crossing before. They said we're to tie ourselves

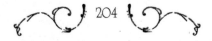

204

to our beds until the storm dies down."

Beth struggled to keep her footing as the deck seesawed beneath her feet. All her combs and brushes fell and rattled across the floor. "Good idea," she panted. "We need to find something to tie ourselves down with."

They found a length of rope that had been tied around one of Beth's many boxes, cut it in half and tied themselves securely to their beds. As Beth lay there with the rope tied tightly, she prayed Ralph was safe. This was a storm like nothing she'd ever heard of before.

Suddenly she stiffened. Something was rattling, and then the handle of her cabin door began to turn…

At the same time, Ralph clung to the sodden rigging, which was prickly as a thorn bush and cold as an icicle in his hands. Wind howled around him, making his teeth rattle. He pulled himself further up the rigging and got a fresh handhold. Two other sailors were swarming up the rigging behind him. If the sails weren't reefed securely, exposing as little surface as possible, the sheer force of the wind would fling the ship about like a toy boat, or even snap a mast in half.

Ralph had always had a good head for heights, but even he felt giddy as he looked down to the tilting deck below. Wave after wave broke over the railings, sending tons of water sluicing over the deck and escaping over the other side in foaming torrents. At times the sea seemed like it would engulf the ship completely, and Ralph bit his lip as he waited for the deck to reappear from under the flood.

"Come on!" he urged himself. The other sailors were close behind him. The wind fought to tear Ralph off the rigging and fling him into the churning sea, but he hung on and kept climbing towards the yard. All sailors had a rule they knew by heart: one hand for yourself, and one for the ship. It meant that whatever job you were doing with one hand, you always hung on with the other. The sail flapping made a sound like harsh thunder, and Ralph knew all too well that wet canvas in a high wind wasn't like cloth at all. It felt more like metal.

He glanced down again, just in time to glimpse a hunched-over figure opening the door to the passenger cabins. Next moment, there was no sign of him. Ralph looked up and down, but the man wasn't clinging to the railings or sprawling on the deck. He'd gone below. Ralph spat a curse. "Go on without me!" he yelled to the

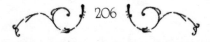

two other sailors. "I'll catch you up!"

The sailors stared down at him in bewildered anger. They must think he was abandoning his post. But there was no time to explain. If Ralph had seen what he thought he'd seen, he had to act quickly.

He scrambled back down the rigging as fast as he could and dashed for the door, with the ship rolling and pitching beneath him. A wave smashed down on the deck just as he threw the door to the cabins open and rushed inside. The man he'd seen was standing in the corridor, turning the handle to Beth's cabin.

"Going somewhere, Shaw?"

Shaw slowly turned to look at him. He let go of the door handle and drew a dagger from his belt.

"I'd turn around if I were you," he said. "Forget you saw anything."

"What's the plan, Shaw? Stab them all to death in their beds, then chuck them overboard?"

Shaw licked his lips. "Serves them right for going up on deck during a storm, don't it? The girl, her maid, and Turner too. I know they're in cahoots. I'll just say I saw them hit by a wave and washed over the side. Nobody will be any the wiser."

"Drop that blade."

Shaw laughed. "Or you'll do what? Don't worry, I'll put you on my little list too. Who are you, anyway? One more of the King's running dogs?"

He began to advance on Ralph, forcing the young man back down the corridor. Ralph could only back away, through the door and out onto the tilting deck. Shaw had murder in his eyes now. Whatever else might happen, he had to kill Ralph and they both knew it. He had seen too much.

"There's two men up in the rigging," Ralph said. "They'll see you."

"Not in this storm they won't!" Shaw snarled. He jabbed at Ralph, nearly cutting flesh. The rain was lashing down hard upon them. Ralph badly needed a weapon – any weapon. He struggled to keep his footing as the ship tilted this way and that, when suddenly an idea struck him. He grabbed for one of the belaying pins – the short wooden rods used to tie ropes off – and pulled it from its hole.

Shaw roared in anger and leaped at him. The dagger sliced down through the air, ripping the cloth of Ralph's soaking jacket, nicking the skin of his chest painfully. But now Shaw was off-balance. Ralph swung at him with the belaying pin and caught him a solid blow

on the temple. Shaw shook himself as watery blood went coursing down his face, into his eye, leaving him half-blind.

"That 'urt," he said, baring his teeth. "Get 'ere, you little—"

Ralph quickly glanced to his right. A huge wave was coming, roaring in from Shaw's blind side. He quickly hooked his arm through the ship's rail, praying this would work.

Shaw came in for the kill, and Ralph was a sitting duck, clinging to the rail like that, unable to dodge. One quick dagger thrust to the chest, perhaps another two for good measure, and he'd be dead.

The wave struck.

An avalanche of water thundered down upon Ralph, stinging like a fist in the face. Salt water burned his eyes, but he held on, sputtering and gasping, his arm in agony, as the sea tried to tear him away. Shaw screamed, and Ralph saw him for the briefest of moments, trying – too late – to grab the rail. The next moment, the deluge had carried him over the side.

As the last of the wave washed past and the ship rocked wearily back again, Ralph looked out to where Shaw was floundering in the open sea. He surfaced once,

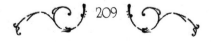

twice – then went under, never to come up again.

"One hand for yourself, chum," Ralph said quietly to himself, "and one for the ship."

Tucking the belaying pin back where it belonged, he went to rejoin his shipmates in the rigging.

Hours later, Beth woke up. Her chest was aching and rubbed raw, but the rope had gone. The grey light of a new day was seeping through the window.

"Maisie?" she whispered.

"I untied you, miss." Maisie handed Beth a hot cup of water laced with warming spices. "Captain says the storm's behind us now, so it was safe to come out again."

Beth drank gratefully. "I thought we'd all be drowned. Are John and Ralph—?"

"They're fine, m'lady," Maisie said, with a meaningful glance that said "remember who you're supposed to be". "Briskell is taking inventory of our belongings, and Ralph has been commended to the captain for his bravery." She hung her head. "But the storm took its toll, just the same."

"How many?" Beth whispered.

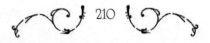

"Three. All sailors. All young men." She paused. "Master Ralph said to tell you that a certain *Shaw* was one of them. He said you'd understand…"

Later, as the passengers and crew gathered on deck to pray for the three drowned sailors, Beth looked to the skies and saw they were clearing. The other passengers saw it too, and the relief on their faces was plain to see. This must be what the very first settlers felt, Beth realized, when they crossed the ocean to reach the New World. The sun's rays fell on her tear-streaked face as once again, she thanked providence that her friends were still with her. There would be other dangers, other storms; but for now, at least, they were together. *For now.*

# Chapter Twenty-Two

## The Far, Fatal Shore

"Land ho!"

Beth and Maisie looked at one another, eyes wide with excitement. After more than two months at sea, after all the storms and seasickness, could they really be here at last?

"Come on!" Beth cried, grabbing Maisie's hand. "Let's go and see!"

People were stampeding out of their cabins and charging up the steps. They made way for Beth, though, not wishing to offend a grand lady. She glided to the railings and peered into the dim distance.

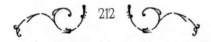

"I can't see anything," Maisie complained. "Maybe it's a false sighting."

The other passengers pressed close around her, all of them trying to see the American coast. Excited conversation babbled from every part of the ship. Captain Clark was up at the helm, shading his eyes from the sun, trying to see. As minutes passed with nobody else seeing the supposed land, Beth's heart began to sink. False sightings were all too common out here at sea, especially after a long voyage. Patches of green sea-scum often looked like land to weary sailors.

Beth narrowed her eyes. Far in the west, below a wisp of low cloud, was a faint but visible patch of light brown. That was no drift of seaweed or algae. That was land.

"Land ho!" she yelled, flinging her arm out as if she were hurling a javelin. "Land ho!"

A cheer went up as everyone looked where she was pointing.

"That's land all right, m'lady," said John. "Your new home."

"And yours," she whispered. "We're here. We made it!"

She wished she could have given him a hug, right then and there, but no lady would ever hug a servant,

especially not one as strict as she'd painted herself to be.

But to her surprise, John reached over, first glancing about to see that nobody was paying attention, and briefly entwined his fingers with hers.

"I … I just want to say," he began in a low voice, "that there's nobody else I'd rather begin this new life with." John's eyes shone with a sincerity that made Beth's heart leap. She squeezed his hand in hers before reluctantly pulling away, her face flushed.

The closer they drew to the American shore, the more detail Beth could make out. At first there was nothing but hills and trees, with no sign of civilization. Maisie had told her to expect this, but the vastness of it all still took her breath away. But as the ship headed upriver towards the docks of Jamestown, she began to see houses. They looked strangely familiar, much like London houses, but out of place – as if some unimaginable force had plucked them up and replanted them thousands of miles away.

"Look there, miss!" Maisie told her. "There's the tobacco fields."

Beth could see them now, long fields stretching away beyond the dock for what looked like miles. Leafy plants grew there in thick bunches, far too many to count.

"It's so different," she said. "There's so much space!

Even the sky seems bigger here."

Soon the dock loomed up ahead, and Beth could make out a crowd gathered there waiting for the ship to land. Faint smells of wood-smoke and cooking bacon reached her nostrils, making her mouth water. Even the air seemed clean. There was none of London's filth and stink here. The New World wasn't yet stained by the hordes of humanity packed into one small place, with drains overflowing and chamber pots emptied into the street. This was a place to make a fresh start and build a spy network that would make Strange proud.

The only question was: how much had Vale already built here?

After such a long voyage, the last ten minutes seemed to take hours. Eventually the *Antelope* was moored and the gangplank lowered. The first-time passengers crowded around, eager to be first onto American soil, while the seasoned travellers stood back and watched in amusement.

"Stand back!" Captain Clark boomed. "Let Lady Easton through! Don't you know how to treat a lady?"

So it was that Beth became the first of the *Antelope*'s passengers to alight at Jamestown. The crowd waiting at the dock rushed up to her eagerly, half of them wanting

to ask her questions and the other half struggling to protect her from the first. Beth felt her legs wobble a little as she finally stepped onto dry land.

"Please, good people, let me through!" she laughed. "It's been a long voyage, and a lady requires her rest!"

"Excuse me, m'lady. Is there word of the *Dreadnought*?" a man demanded. "Have you sighted her?"

"Uh, I'm afraid not," Beth said, curious by what he meant. "Now, if you'll excuse me…"

Another man pushed forwards. "Was she wrecked? They say a spar was washed ashore!"

"Please, ask Captain Clark!" she said. Somehow she needed to get rid of these eager townsfolk. She pressed her hand to her forehead. "I feel faint."

"Room!" roared a bearded man in a long smock. "Give the lady room, blast you! Can't you see she knows nothing of the damn ship? Let's ask the captain like she said!"

Beth and Maisie pushed out of the other side of the crowds, who by now were pestering the other passengers for information. The *Dreadnought* was the name on everyone's lips. John came staggering behind, laden down with the luggage.

"We need to find our new house," Beth said. "By the look of it, it's up that hill. Good lord, look at those

buildings! The size of them!"

"Almost as big as your uncle's mansion in Oxford, my lady," said John pointedly.

Beth coughed. "Yes. Quite. Well, let's be off. Did you speak to that young chap – what was his name? Ralph?"

"Indeed I did, ma'am. He's keen to enter your employ, and will join us as soon as he has discharged his duties on board ship."

"I'm ruddy starving," Maisie muttered under her breath. "I keep smelling food! Can't we stop at that chop-house before we go?"

"I don't think grand ladies eat at chop-houses," Beth muttered back, though her own stomach was achingly empty. Then she turned back. "Oh, the devil with it. If a grand lady can't eat wherever she likes then what's the point of being one?"

The owner of Whitworth's Chop House was flabbergasted that Lady Easton had chosen to dine at his humble establishment, and told her so several times over. To Beth's surprise, the other patrons seemed to like her all the better for it.

"This is America!" one of them proudly said. "See? She understands! She ain't going around with her nose in the air like she's too good for us!"

Soon they were eagerly devouring the first fresh meat they'd had in months, with Beth at a table by the window and John and Maisie at the back of the place. Beth decided that keeping her mouth shut was the best option. The less people knew about her, the more interesting she'd be to them. So she ate in silence while people whispered behind their hands.

"How did you know Lady Easton was coming to Jamestown?" John asked the owner. "That's quite a crowd out there."

"Oh, that crowd's not for her," the man said. "They're all waiting for news of the *Dreadnought*. She's a convict ship, out of Plymouth."

John felt a chill when he heard the words "convict ship". "I don't see why they'd be so interested in England's garbage," he said, trying to stay calm.

"Then you don't know how things work around here," said the man, settling onto a chair beside John. "All those people are businessmen, plantation owners and homesteaders. They need able-bodied men to work for them. Those convicts are free labour, for as long as their sentences last."

Outside, the crowd was dispersing. The plantation owners were grumbling to one another.

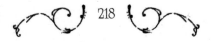

218

"Doesn't look like the news was good," John said.

"Rumours were true, then," said the chop-house owner. "Can't say I'm surprised. The *Dreadnought* was in a bad state of repair, by all accounts. One good sea storm would sink her like a rock. Excuse me." He stood up to welcome in some businessmen who had come in to gawp at Beth and complain about their bad luck. John sat shivering, no longer able to eat his food.

"What's wrong?" Maisie said.

"Didn't you hear? *Dreadnought* was a convict ship, sounds like it's been wrecked." *And I was supposed to be on it*, he added to himself. John remembered the faces of the men who had trudged miserably onto the boats ahead of him. All dead now, along with the guards and the crew. He thought of white faces beneath the water, staring eyes and open mouths.

*Beth and Ralph saved my life*, he thought with a shudder.

As the group finished their meal, a red-faced dockhand peered in through the window, saw Beth and came to speak to them.

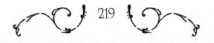

"Pardon me, m'lady, but you didn't ship any unmarked boxes on the *Antelope* with you, by any chance?"

"I only brought clothes and a few personal effects," Beth said politely. "Why, is something the matter?"

"It's the oddest thing," said the man. "There's a load of boxes been unloaded, and none of them have any labels on. Nobody seems to have taken charge of them. Good quality trunks, though, which is why I thought of you. Haven't seen the like since the *Dorcas* came to port a week ago."

"I'd better come and have a look," Beth said, carefully keeping her voice neutral. As the man led the way, she whispered to John "The *Dorcas*! Those trunks have to be Vale's!"

"And Shaw would have been the one to take charge of what he'd loaded onto our boat," John whispered back. "But he's out of the picture…"

"Exactly. So all we need to do is wait for whoever comes to collect the goods, then follow them! It's our first lead!"

"And we've only been here for half an hour," John said with a smile. "You *are* good!"

Beth narrowed her eyes. *We're coming for you, Vale*, she thought to herself. *Ready or not…*

In a mansion on a plantation not far from Jamestown, a crimson chair stood by a window. It was exquisitely made and upholstered in soft leather, but that wasn't why Sir Henry Vale valued it. This was his favourite thinking chair. He had hatched so many murderous schemes while reclining in it that the cushions ought to leak blood. Being without it had been like missing a limb. Now it was finally here in his new base of operations – along with some vital weaponry and documents that he'd need for his on-going ... endeavours. The captain of the *Antelope* had unknowingly carried them over the Atlantic for him, allowing him legitimate distance in case of any unwanted prying or discovery. It wasn't hard to persuade a common sailor to smuggle things on board a ship for you. All it took was money, and Vale had plenty of that.

He lowered himself into the thinking chair as if it had been a hot bath and looked out over his land. Thousands of tobacco plants grew there, flourishing in the Virginia soil – the source of his wealth. He allowed himself a moment of self-congratulation. He, with his brilliant mind, had had the foresight to buy land here when others

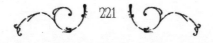

scoffed. He had planted tobacco, despite the merchants' insistence that the fad for smoking would soon pass. Then, when the crop had made him a rich man, he had invested in ships until he had amassed a fleet of his own. Other crop-growers, formerly neighbours and equals, now paid him to transport their goods.

Vale frowned in irritation, remembering the news that had come from the port along with his furniture and goods: he now had one ship fewer. The *Dreadnought* was lost, sunk beyond recovery. His fingers sank into the chair's scarlet leather as if he was clawing out a heart. He hoped Captain Tucker had died screaming. The man deserved no less for his stupidity and incompetence. How *dare* he throw away one of Vale's careful investments like that?

But he soon relaxed again. It was only money, after all. The gold wasn't important. What mattered was the power it gave him. Power to achieve the one thing he truly craved.

He turned a gold sovereign over in his fingers and glared at the image of the King's head. He imagined that head severed from the body. He thought of his own fingers grasping it by the hair, lifting it, displaying it to his loyal followers. He mouthed the words he knew so

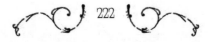

well and meant to say one day soon: *Behold the head of a traitor.*

The King's wretched spies would not reach him here in the New World, he'd seen to that. He had the space and the freedom he needed. Now, at last, it was time to concoct the ultimate murder plan.

He leaned back in his blood-red chair and whispered to himself: "Let us begin…"

# Epilogue

"More cooled tea, m'lady?"

Beth turned around, drawing her eyes away from the plantation that stretched out before her.

"No, thank you, Miss Blanchet," she said, grinning at Maisie. It still took some getting used to, being treated as a lady. "But please, with this warm weather, you must have some for yourself…"

"Thank you, m'lady," Maisie said, returning her smile. "Though I have to say, I like this warmth. Trumps London's fog any day!"

Beth drew in a long breath as Maisie left the veranda.

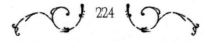

She had to agree – and along with the humidity, the air here still felt abuzz with possibility and excitement, even a month after their arrival. She'd already begun enquiries into purchasing a building in the nearby town to turn into a theatre with her newfound funds, and she was sure to find some local talent to start creating her new company. She already had Maisie as a burgeoning talent, of course…

But more important than that, she, John and Ralph were already hot on the trail of Vale's new "enterprise" here in America. There had been reports of growing disloyalty to the King and his rule in the Colonies in the nearby plantations – and Beth was certain who was behind it. The notorious anti-royalist was playing a long game, trying to cause unrest in the King's empire overseas. *He failed to overthrow His Majesty from within, and now he thinks he can do it from without?* Beth clenched her teeth at the very thought, but then jumped as she heard more footsteps behind her.

"Lady Easton?" The footsteps grew closer, and the voice lowered. "Beth?"

Beth felt heat rise in her cheeks as she turned to see John's handsome face. It was so rare now that her friends got to use her real name; it made her warm inside when

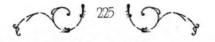

he did so. But as she saw some of the plantation hands heading towards the house for refreshments, she took a step away from him, and John straightened up, handing her a letter more formally.

"This came for you today, m'lady," he said, and she took it. "It's from your family lawyer, Carstairs." He looked at her pointedly.

Beth quickly opened the envelope and, making sure the workers were out of sight now, held it up to the bright sky. Pinpricks. It was a coded message from Strange, replying to her reports about their lead on Vale.

"Go and fetch Ralph," she whispered to John. "We have a plan to put together."

John nodded and went quickly to find their friend amongst the plantation workers.

Beth studied the letter again carefully, nodding intently. She knew Sir Henry Vale would not give up his mission to overthrow the King easily. But if Beth had learned one thing about herself on all the adventures she'd had with her friends and fellow spies so far, it was that the King's elite did not give up easily either.

Vale would pay – she, Ralph and John would make sure of it. And after that? She looked out at the new world around her.

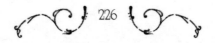

"Endless possibilities…" she whispered to herself with a determined smile.

# ∼ Cast of Characters ∽

### BETH JOHNSON
Actress extraordinaire at the King's Theatre and –
unbeknownst to her admiring audience – a
much-valued spy. Tall and beautiful with chestnut
brown hair and green eyes, Beth has risen from lowly
depths as a foundling abandoned on the steps of Bow
Church to become a celebrated thespian and talented
espionage agent.

### SIR ALAN STRANGE
Tall, dark and mysterious, spymaster Alan Strange
seeks out candidates from all walks of life, spotting the
potential for high-quality agents in the most unlikely
of places. Ruthless but fair, Strange is an inspiration for
his recruits, and trains them well.

### RALPH CHANDLER
Former street urchin Ralph has lead a rough-and-
tumble existence, but his nefarious beginnings have
their uses when employed in his role as one of Sir Alan
Strange's spies, working in the service of the King.

### JOHN TURNER

Junior clerk at the Navy Board, handsome John imagines himself in more daring, adventurous circumstances – and he soon has the opportunity when he meets Beth Johnson and becomes part of her gang of spies.

### SIR HENRY VALE

Criminal mastermind and anti-King conspirator, Sir Henry Vale was supposedly executed by beheading in 1662 for his attempt to take the King's life – but all may not be as it seems…

### EDMUND GROBY

Squat, swarthy and with one ominous finger missing from his left hand, Groby is a relentless villain and loyal henchman. He hates the monarchy and all it represents, and will stop at nothing to prevent our gang from derailing the King-killer's plans.

### MAISIE WHITE

A young orange-seller at the theatre where Beth works, Maisie has been quickly taken under the older girl's wing – but she knows nothing of her friend's double life as a spy…

Dear Reader,

I hope you have enjoyed this book. While Beth Johnson and her friends are fictitious characters, the world that they inhabit is based on history.

Today, if a person is convicted of a crime, they might be fined a sum of money or sent to prison. However, in the past, it was less common to be sent to prison. Instead, criminals could expect to be fined or whipped as a punishment. Many people were sentenced to death, even for crimes that might not seem very serious today.

In the 17th century, the English government began transporting criminals to its new colony in North America, as an alternative to sentencing them to death. The transported criminals then had to serve their sentences by working as forced labour for either seven or fourteen years, depending on the seriousness of their crime. Most transportees never returned home.

In the 1660s, the colony of North America was still in its infancy, and life could be very hard for the people who lived there. However, for many, it also offered freedom and a new beginning.

*Jo Macauley*

Look out for more
Secrets & Spies adventures…

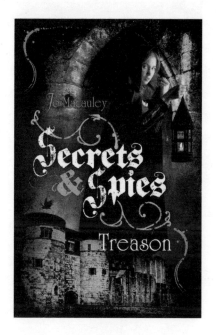

## Treason

The year is 1664, and somebody wants the King dead.
One November morning, a mysterious ghost ship drifts
up the Thames. Sent to investigate, fourteen-year-old
Beth quickly finds herself embroiled in a dangerous
adventure that takes her right into the Tower of
London. Will Beth be able to unravel the plot to kill
the King before it's too late?

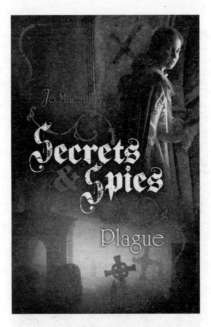

## Plague

A terrible plague is sweeping through London, and Beth and her company of actors are sent to Oxford to entertain the King's court, which has decamped to avoid the deadly disease. However, Beth soon finds herself recalled to London by spymaster Alan Strange, and together with her friends and fellow spies, she must uncover a conspiracy that is taking advantage of the turmoil in the capital. A conspiracy that leads right to the seat of power…

## Inferno

The year is 1666 and Beth is throwing herself into a new dramatic role a the theatre when the kidnapping of fellow spy John's sister pulls her back into fighting the conspiracy against the King. Henry Vale's thugs aim to blackmail John into exposing the King, and Beth and her friends face a race against time to rescue the young girl – and escape the raging fire that threatens to consume the whole city…

For more exciting books from brilliant
authors, follow the fox!
**www.curious-fox.com**